Hi there,

I just wanted to say hello and tell you a bit about myself.

I live on the very outside of London near the River Thames, with my husband (who is Dutch and makes great pancakes!) and our two young daughters. We also have a Siamese cat called Hamish who came to us as a very timid rescue cat and spent the first few weeks hiding up the chimney! Now he is a real family cat and loves sitting on my lap (and trying to sit on my keyboard!) when I'm at my desk writing.

I'm half Welsh and half English but I grew up in Scotland. Before I became a writer I worked as a doctor, mainly with children and teenagers. From as far back as I can remember I've always loved stories in any form – reading books, watching films, playing make-believe games. As a child I always had one fantasy world or another on the go and as I grew older that changed to actual ongoing sagas that I wrote down in exercise books and worked on for weeks at a time.

I really hope you enjoy reading this – and that you'll write to me at **Gwyneth.Rees@bloomsbury.com** to let me know what you think. I'd love it if you told me a bit about yourself too!

Best wishes,

Books by Gwyneth Rees

Coming soon:

The Honeymoon Sisters

For younger readers:

The *Fairy Dust* series

Cosmo and the Magic Sneeze

The Magic Princess Dress

My Super Sister

My Super Sister and the Birthday Party

CHERRY BLOSSOM DREAMS

CHERRY BLOSSOM DREAMS

Gwyneth Rees

BLOOMSBURY
LONDON   NEW DELHI   NEW YORK   SYDNEY

Bloomsbury Publishing, London, New Delhi, New York and Sydney

First published in Great Britain in June 2015 by Bloomsbury Publishing Plc
50 Bedford Square, London WC1B 3DP

www.bloomsbury.com

Bloomsbury is a registered trademark of Bloomsbury Publishing Plc

A CIP catalogue record for this book is available from the British Library

ISBN 978 1 4088 5263 7

Typeset by RefineCatch Limited, Bungay, Suffolk
Printed and bound in Great Britain by CPI Group (UK) Ltd, Croydon CR0 4YY

1 3 5 7 9 10 8 6 4 2

In memory of Karen Cheylan
29th April 1974 – 17th April 2014

Chapter One

To be honest, I was feeling a bit nervous about telling Lily my big news. It's not that I don't trust her. After all, she's my best friend and I know she's always got my back, even if lately it seems like all she's interested in is boys, fashion, soap operas and more boys. It was just that this was such a Big Thing and the consequences if she did spill the beans – especially at school – would be massive. And I'm not just talking a little bit massive. I'm talking volcano-erupting massive here.

'So tell me *everything*!' demanded Lily, closing her bedroom door as I went over to flop down on her bed. I hadn't seen her this excited since I'd first dished out the news that Mum was dating our English teacher, Mr Anderson.

Or *Leo* as we call him now (except when we're in school, of course).

'I can't believe you guys actually went *on holiday* with him!' Lily dived on to the end of her bed like she used to do when we were much younger. Lily and I have been best friends since we were in the infants. Now that we're older – Lily is already thirteen and I will be too in a couple of months – we aren't really in the same classes and we don't hang out together much in school. But the two of us still see each other in the holidays and at the weekends. 'This is way beyond cool, Sasha,' Lily informed me. 'This is like the most amazing thing that's *ever* happened to a kid in our school!'

'Don't be daft!' I snapped. Lily tends to exaggerate when she gets excited about something – and my mum and our English teacher (who is generally considered to be pretty hot) spending the Easter holiday together in Greece with me and my twin brother, Sean, as witnesses, had to be ... well ... the most exciting thing ever to happen in our little town as far as she was concerned.

'So *spill*,' she said. 'Don't miss out a single detail. I bet he looks great in swimming trunks, doesn't he?'

'*Lily!*' I hissed, feeling myself flushing.

'You do realise your mother's a total cradle snatcher?' Lily declared. 'Don't look like that! It wasn't a criticism.

We're all dead impressed that she's got herself a boyfriend ten years younger than her. My mum says good on her and even my gran said "Way to go" when Mum told her you were all going on holiday together!'

'He's only *nine* years younger and you promised not to tell anyone!' I suddenly imagined her entire extended family sharing the news about Mum and Leo with the whole planet on Facebook.

'I thought you just meant don't tell anyone at school. I don't know why you want to keep it a secret though. It's nothing to be ashamed of. After all, Leo is a total H.O.G.!'

'Huh?' I looked at her blankly.

'Hot Older Guy,' Lily elaborated impatiently. Lily can be pretty embarrassing the way she talks about guys sometimes. Mostly her crushes are on pop stars or famous actors, but just occasionally she gets one on an unobtainable person in real life instead.

I don't think she has a proper crush on Leo but with Lily you can never be a hundred per cent sure. 'Come on then,' she prompted. 'Tell me what happened!'

'Well . . .' I began. 'Actually I've got some *really* big news but Mum wants to keep it a secret for now. I'll tell *you* as long as you promise not to tell anyone else –

seriously, Lily, not *anyone*. OK? Not your mum or your granny or your auntie or your cousins and definitely not anyone in our school.'

'OK, OK, I promise,' Lily said. 'You know you can trust me with a real secret.'

'Well . . . Mum and Leo got *engaged* on holiday.'

Lily practically screamed. 'No way! You mean he actually proposed? Did he get down on one knee? Did he already have the ring? Tell me everything, Sasha – and I mean *everything*! Oh my God, this is awesome!' Lily is a bit of a drama queen in case you hadn't noticed. In fact her mum says 'hyperbole' is her middle name (I had to look it up, but she's right).

Actually, it was Mum who proposed to Leo. But Leo said yes straight away and went out and bought her a ring from a little jewellery shop in the seaside village where we were staying. And now me and my brother are going to have Mr Anderson as our step-dad. And no one at school – absolutely no one – is allowed to know. At least not until Leo has worked out how to tell our head teacher, Mr Jamieson.

'You know Clara has a major crush on him, don't you? She'll be so jealous!'

'No, Lily! You promised not to tell anyone at school!'
I said fiercely.

'I don't mean *now*, but eventually, when people find
out. I mean, they will have to know some day, won't
they? They'll be having a wedding! You can't do that in
secret.'

I muttered something under my breath.

Lily frowned. 'What?'

'I said *if* it actually happens. This is *Mum* we're talking
about here.'

Lily shook her head at me. 'You're such a pessimist,
Sasha. This is, like, the best thing that's happened to you
in *forever* . . . and you've got to be all gloom and doom
straight away.'

'I'm just being realistic,' I said hotly. 'Mum's always
been unlucky when it comes to love. Even Granny says so
and she doesn't even believe in luck and fate and stuff
like that.'

'Unlucky? You mean because your dad died?' Lily
sounded genuinely puzzled before adding quickly, 'I
know that *was* pretty unlucky, but –'

'It's not just that,' I told her. 'Mum is always falling in
love with the wrong people! Remember when she met
Gambling Gordon?'

'How could I forget Gee-Gee?' Lily said with a grin. She was especially proud of her pet name for the boyfriend who was always borrowing money off Mum to bet on the horses. 'That didn't last long. What was it? Six months, tops? Your mum's not *that* daft!'

'I know, but then there was Married Michael . . .'

Lily had named him that in retrospect. Mum had met Michael when Sean and I were nine (four years after our dad died) and we had all really liked him. After he had been in our lives for a whole year we found out that he didn't actually travel a lot for work as he'd always claimed, but that he had a wife and kids in another part of the country. Mum had been devastated. I still can't think of that time without getting butterflies in my tummy.

'I'm telling you, Mum is totally jinxed when it comes to romance,' I told Lily. 'So I don't want to get too excited about Leo just yet, OK?'

Lily sighed. 'But this is different. She's been dating Leo for over a year and they knew each other way before that, the whole time he was tutoring Sean. They've actually had a chance to really get to know each other. Sean trusts him, doesn't he?'

I nodded. Sean thought the world of Leo. It had been Sean's Year Five teacher who had first encouraged Mum to employ Leo as a tutor, saying that my brother was a lot more capable academically than he let on. (I've always worked hard and done well at school without needing any extra help – a fact which I sometimes think Mum doesn't appreciate enough.)

Anyway, thanks to Leo, Sean had managed to get through the entrance exam for Helensfield High (the grammar school just down the road from us), where Leo is one of the English teachers. And later, when Sean had been struggling to cope with Year Seven, Mum had asked Leo to come and give him some more help. Mum was single again at that point and Leo had started staying for a drink and a chat with Mum after Sean's lesson was over.

Now my brother and I were about to start our final term of Year Eight I could hardly believe that Mum and Leo had been dating for more than a year. I mean, it's pretty weird seeing your teacher in his dressing gown, knowing what his favourite pizza is and even seeing him snog your mum on the odd occasion you walk in on them and they can't jump apart quickly enough. But we'd eventually started to get used to it, and I was getting so accustomed to Leo being around at home that I had even stopped noticing how good-looking he is. Until someone like Lily draws attention to it, that is.

'Right then, so it's just *you* that's being all negative as usual,' Lily concluded.

'It's not just me! Granny's worried too,' I pointed out, thinking how right my grandmother's instincts had been where Married Michael was concerned. In fact our grandmother had once told Mum that maybe she should stop looking for love and concentrate on bringing up me and my brother instead. That had gone down like a ton of bricks, because if there's one thing Mum can't stand it's the thought of staying single for the rest of her life.

'Yeah, well, she's *meant* to worry,' Lily responded impatiently. '*She's* an old lady. You're not, in case you hadn't noticed. Honestly, why can't you just lighten up and enjoy life for once?'

'I *do* enjoy life!'

'No, you don't. You're so cautious, Sasha. You never do anything outside your comfort zone.'

I sighed loudly. I should have known she would turn the conversation round to this. It was getting to be a recurring topic with Lily, who wanted me to do more stuff with her and her new friends outside school. Frankly, her persistence about it was starting to get on my nerves. Why should I like all the same things they liked? I decided to try a new tactic.

8

'So what's wrong with that? I *like* my comfort zone. It's . . . well . . . *comforting*!' I gave her a grin to cajole her but her frown didn't budge.

'Look, Sasha,' she went on with feeling, 'you're practically a teenager and you don't act the least bit like one. You're not even interested in clothes. Look at you – you've got a really great figure and yet you dress like . . . well . . . like you want to hide it or something.'

I just gaped at her because this was over the top even for Lily.

'Who's got a great figure?' said a teasing male voice. I nearly died of embarrassment when Lily's fifteen-year-old brother Rafferty – or Raffy as everybody calls him – pushed open the door and stuck his head round. He was wearing jeans with a tight black T-shirt on his top half. I couldn't help staring at his chest and thinking that it was quite a bit more muscly than my brother's. It was then that I found myself beginning to blush.

I stood up in a rush and made a grab for my big baggy cardy that was lying on Lily's bed. 'I'd better go,' I muttered. I couldn't bring myself to brush past Rafferty, who was still watching the two of us from the doorway, looking amused.

'She's right. You *do* have a nice figure,' he told me with a grin. I'm sure my face was like a beetroot by then, and my palms felt clammy. 'I mean, a lot of girls your age still have loads of puppy fat – like Lily here.'

'*WHAT?*' Lily screamed, hurling a shoe at him. 'I HATE YOU! GET OUT OF MY ROOM RIGHT NOW!'

As she picked up a second shoe I made my escape, not looking back as I bolted down their stairs, shouting, 'See you at school!'

Chapter Two

As I walked back from Lily's house clutching my cardigan round me protectively, I kept thinking about what she had said about me having a nice figure. On holiday we had mainly been sightseeing, but on a couple of warm, sunny days we had gone to the beach. I had worn a bikini until a boy who was slightly older had wolf-whistled at me. I don't know why, but it made me feel really uncomfortable. After that I had made sure I kept my T-shirt on the whole time. I'd never thought much about what I looked like on the beach before. I mean, I've never been fat, and it wasn't like my shape had changed *that* much in other ways yet, but the bikini sort of emphasised what little change there was, I suppose.

I'm certainly not as developed on top as Lily, who has already started her periods. When I mentioned to Mum that I wished I would hurry up and start mine, she laughed and told me that the day would come soon enough. Mum started when she was eleven – the same as Lily – so she doesn't know what it's like having to wait and worry about it. I'll be thirteen in a few months, so it's got to happen soon and the whole thing is stressing me out. What if it happens when I'm at school? Will everyone know? Will it be really embarrassing? Will it hurt? I'm one of the youngest in our year and Lily makes me feel like such a baby if I try and discuss it with her. Mum doesn't help either. She says that since she's totally forgotten where she was (or how she felt) when she started her very first period, then it couldn't have been all that traumatic. And she just rolls her eyes at me impatiently when I point out that people sometimes completely suppress their memories of *really* traumatic childhood events.

My feet suddenly felt a bit chilly and I looked down at the silver and blue flip-flops I'd bought in Greece. Now that I was back home I didn't want to stop wearing them, but I had to admit that mid-April at home was a lot cooler than in Greece.

Fleetingly I wished we were still on holiday. We'd had the best time ever with Leo there to keep Mum in a good mood and to make us all laugh. As we explored the ancient Greek temples and other historical sites, he kept joking that it made him feel like he was in an Indiana Jones adventure, except that there were no baddies.

Mum kept saying that it was wonderful to watch Sean and Leo getting on so well together. Mum always says that not having a dad is especially hard on Sean because it means he has no positive male role model (our grandfathers both died before we were born). I try not to let it bug me that she never appears so concerned that *I* don't have a dad. Her take on daughters seems to be that if they have a mother then that's good enough, with a dad being a kind of very nice luxury. I know Mum didn't see much of her own father when she was growing up – not because he was dead like ours, but because he was always away at work. But she tells me this as if it therefore follows that it's no big deal for *me* not to have a dad, which is actually pretty hurtful because really it's a *massive* deal, especially when I see how protective and proud Lily's dad is of her. And the way Mum doesn't seem to get that is just . . . well, *horrible*. In fact it sometimes makes me feel like I don't have much of a mum either – not one who bothers trying to understand me, at any rate.

When I got home, Mum was in the hall doing yoga. It wasn't odd for her to be doing yoga, but it *was* odd for her to be doing it in the hall where anyone could trip over her.

'Mum, do you think I've got a nice figure?' I asked, even though I know I'm not meant to speak to her if she's in the lotus position with her eyes closed.

Mum has a *really* nice figure. She's tall and slim – but not too slim as she's always quick to point out (she's never approved of all those size zero models and she's always telling me how important it is for a woman to have some curves). She has long, straight black hair, pale skin and very striking blue eyes. When I was little I used to think she looked just like Snow White.

'You *will* have,' she answered, opening her eyes to look at me, 'when you fill out a bit.'

'Fill out a bit?'

'In the right places, I mean.' She sighed and shifted position on the floor. Clearly she hadn't been properly into her meditation. 'Why? What has Lily been saying about your figure?'

'Nothing . . . it doesn't matter . . . Mum, since when did you try to meditate in the *hall*?'

'It wasn't planned, Sasha. I was about to phone your grandmother and I suddenly thought it might help if I tried to centre myself first. But I think where Granny is concerned, my anxious thoughts are meditation-resistant!' She stood up, smiling at her own joke. 'Now you know, Sasha, that girls go through puberty at different rates and just because Lily has already –'

'Mum, stop it!' I said, feeling embarrassed. 'It's not that. It's –'

But then Sean walked into the hall and I shut up abruptly. There was no way I was continuing this discussion with him listening. Not that my brother has got anything to celebrate yet as far as adolescent development goes. OK, so he's nice enough to look at, I suppose – like me, Sean has our father's brown hair and brown eyes, and sometimes when you look at a photo of our dad it's like imagining Sean when he's grown up – but he's pretty small for his age. We were born prematurely – apparently that happens sometimes with twins – and Sean was the smaller out of the two of us. Even now, people who don't know us tend to assume he's my younger brother, which drives him mad.

'Haven't you done it yet?' Sean asked Mum, sounding impatient.

'Do I *look* like I've done it?' she snapped.

'Come on, Mum – stop procrastinating,' Sean said.

Mum glared at him. 'I didn't realise you even *knew* such a big word.'

Sean grinned. 'Blame Leo. He's on a mission to improve my vocabulary. But come on, Mum. If you're going to tell Granny you're engaged, you might as well get it over with. Stop panicking. It'll be fine.'

I just looked at him. *Fine?* Was he crazy?

As you've probably worked out already, Sean and I are very different in some ways. I've always been the sensible one. I like to think things through and make the right decision. I hate getting into any kind of trouble and Mum's always been able to rely on me when she needs someone to lean on. Sean, on the other hand, is a bit of a show-off. He likes to play the clown and he always has the ability to make people laugh, even when things are tough. Unlike me, Sean definitely *isn't* a worrier.

For example, if someone says something bitchy to me in school, I'll spend that whole evening stressing about it, whereas if that happens to Sean, he'll say the other person is an idiot (or worse) and forget about the whole thing in five seconds flat.

There are times though, when I reckon it is just being realistic to be worried sick about something – like *now*, for example. I mean, if you'd met my granny you'd totally get the whole emergency meditation thing. You see, Granny always has an opinion and she invariably thinks it's her duty to pass it on in its purest form.

Her reaction when Mum had first started dating Leo was typical. 'Are you seriously telling me he's only *twenty-eight*? You have to be out of your mind, Annabel! You need a boyfriend who can be a father figure to the children – not one who can double up as their playmate!'

Ouch!

Oh yes – I could well imagine the horribly tactless and offensive things Granny would say to Mum now.

'The trouble with Granny is that she's way too honest,' I said with a sigh.

Mum nodded. 'It wouldn't be so bad if only she'd impart her opinions with just a modicum of sugar coating.'

I nodded again. But even though that is definitely true, I don't want you to get the idea that Granny's *all* bad. OK, so Mum and her have always argued a lot – mainly because Granny is so bossy and thinks she knows what's best for everybody. But whenever Mum's feeling very low, she'll still phone her to ask for her advice – and then get upset when Granny dishes out far too much of it. The thing is, whenever Mum is *really* in trouble, it's always Granny who comes to the rescue. She practically *lived* with us for the first year after we lost our dad and she also stayed with us a lot during the first few months after Mum split up with Michael. And I have to admit that it was very comforting back then to believe that Granny always knew what to do, because I don't remember ever feeling that way about Mum after our dad died.

'Mum, you can always let Granny find out later,' I suggested now.

'Yes, Mum,' Sean added. 'It's not like she's going to congratulate you in any case. All she'll do is freak out and launch into her "toy boy" speech again . . .'

'That's enough advice from you, Sean,' Mum responded sharply. 'And you'd better drop the word "toy boy" from your vocabulary, young man. You know the effect it had on Leo the last time he heard you use it.'

Sean went all sulky then, like he always does when he gets reminded of that. The thing about my brother is that even though he acts like he doesn't care about anything half the time, as soon as you get to really know him you find out that there are a few things – and people – that he cares about massively.

I first realised Leo was one of them six months ago when I saw a side of my brother that I hadn't seen in quite a while.

It began one Friday evening when Mum arrived home from work. We'd just started to realise that Mum and Leo were getting serious, and he was spending more and more time at our house.

'Hey, Mum, how does it feel to have a toy boy?' Sean greeted her jokily the second she walked in through the front door.

Unfortunately she wasn't alone. Leo was right behind her. His expression turned icy cold.

My brother immediately blushed so awfully that his entire face went pink and both of his ears turned bright red. 'Sorry . . .' he mumbled, looking like he might be about to throw up. And that was when I first realised how important Leo was to him.

For the rest of the evening, Leo stayed cool towards Sean. He went home really early, which Mum blamed on Sean, making my brother feel even worse. When Leo came back the following lunchtime, Sean made a more direct attempt to engage him.

'I'm just doing my English homework, Leo,' he said. 'Please can I ask you a question about it?'

Normally Leo would have been delighted to see my brother taking his homework so seriously. And he'd have been more than happy to switch back into tutor mode for a bit.

But instead he gave Sean a reprimanding sort of look. 'I think you should be trying harder to do your homework on your own, Sean,' he stated crisply. 'Perhaps if you tried keeping your bottom on your chair and your eyes on the page in front of you for longer than a few minutes at a time, you'd actually find you could do it by yourself.'

Sean was totally humiliated and he beat a hasty retreat to his bedroom. Even Mum looked a bit surprised by the put-down, though she didn't say anything.

Much later that day, after Leo had relaxed and watched one of his favourite films on the sofa with Mum, he went upstairs to talk to my brother, and things were fine afterwards.

But by that time I had come to understand two things I hadn't realised before. First, maybe Mum was right about Sean wanting a father figure. And second, Leo was clearly hugely embarrassed and uncomfortable about the age gap between Mum and him. And we were going to have to keep our mouths firmly zipped on that subject from now on if we wanted to keep him in our lives.

Chapter Three

I may not be confident and sophisticated like Lily, or good at making people laugh like Sean, but the one thing I've always been able to do well is work out what people are feeling, even when they try to hide it. For instance, I can always tell when Mum is starting to feel down, or when she's scared and trying to pretend she isn't, or when she secretly hates whoever it is she's talking to (which is surprisingly often).

When Mum finally plucked up the courage to phone Granny and acted disappointed when Granny didn't pick up, I knew that she was actually relieved. I had to prompt her to leave a message asking Granny to phone back.

We live in the same town where Mum grew up, but Granny sold that house after she retired and moved away to live in a bungalow by the sea. It's just as well really, since Mum and Granny get on best when they see each other in small doses.

'I'm going out now,' Sean announced as Mum put down the phone.

'Where?' Mum asked.

'Blossom House,' said Sean.

Mum works as an estate agent, and Blossom House is one of the houses on her list. 'Why?' she asked.

'I want to take some new photos.' Sean was looking a bit shifty and I was pretty sure there was more to it than that.

'Do we *need* new photos?' Mum sounded surprised.

'Well, the last ones were taken before the blossom came out, and the light at the back of the house should be perfect right now.'

'That's true, I suppose,' Mum agreed, looking out of the window. One thing about Mum is that she's really good at her job. She always likes to wait until the weather is just right before going to take photos of the houses she's trying to sell, and she always makes sure the pictures are up to date. She says it was our dad who got her doing that because he was massively into photography. Our house is full of photos of us as babies, of Mum looking beautiful, of moody and dramatic shots of the sea and trees and landscapes from all around the world. There are some older family photos too: one of Mum's father in his magician's costume, another one of him and Mum together, a couple of my mum and dad at university and one of Granny as a teenager, wearing a massive feathery hat.

Anyway, whenever a new house gets taken on Mum's books, she'll dash out to take pictures of it just after breakfast if that's when the sun is going to be on the front, and return in the evening if that's when the light will look best at the back. When we were younger, Mum often had to take Sean and me with her and she started to let us take some photos too. Sean is really good at it now and Mum sometimes ends up using his shots instead of hers. Mum's boss doesn't mind. In fact she was the first to tell Sean he must have inherited his talent from our dad.

Sean went to fetch his camera – an expensive one that had belonged to our dad, which Mum had let him keep.

I watched him closely as he returned with it and opened the drawer where Mum keeps all the keys for her houses. I still had the feeling he was up to something. But *what*?

'Don't take the whole bunch, Sean,' Mum instructed him. 'Take off the key to the side gate – that's all you need. And make sure you lock it again when you leave.'

'I have done this before, Mum,' Sean said impatiently, just as the phone started ringing.

'Granny!' we all announced at once.

But one look at the caller display told us it was Leo.

'I think I'll go with Sean,' I whispered as Mum picked up the phone, and Mum nodded as I slipped out through the front door behind my brother.

Just so you know, Mum would never normally let us take photographs of any of the houses on her list without her being present. But Blossom House has been empty for well over two years, ever since its elderly owner died, and it's only a five-minute walk from where we live. And of course Mum has no idea that we've ever let ourselves inside the house itself . . .

'Haven't you got anything better to do?' Sean asked me as I did my best to keep up with him in my flip-flops.

'Hey, it's my house too,' I told him indignantly.

I expect that sounds weird, but at some point in the past two years we had definitely started feeling as if Blossom House belonged to us. Sean had even had an extra set of keys cut, without telling Mum of course.

Mum says that she's always loved houses and that's why she became an estate agent. I'm beginning to think that might run in our family because I'd definitely fallen head-over-heels in love with Blossom House. It sounds crazy, right? Most girls my age are either madly in love with some guy, or with their pony or with the lead singer in their favourite boy band. But stupid or not, it just happened. There was something about Blossom House that drew me in – right from the very first moment I clapped eyes on it.

I'll never forget the first time Mum took us inside.

It was during the Easter holidays two years ago. Miranda, Mum's boss, had asked her to check up on a window that she thought might have been left open. It was a couple of weeks after Mum had found out the truth about Married Michael and she wasn't in a very good state. Mum had already talked to me a lot about how awful she felt, and part of me was glad because it made me feel closer to her. But the other part wished she wouldn't tell me quite so much, because sometimes the things she said scared me.

Blossom House was a big detached three-storey Victorian building that had been allowed to fall into a pretty bad state. But on the day we first saw it the magnolia tree in the front garden was in full bloom and all I noticed as we walked down the drive was the gorgeous pinky-white blossom.

'That tree needs cutting down,' Mum grunted. 'It blocks out all the light.'

I gaped at her. I didn't contradict her though, because when she wasn't confiding in me she'd been snapping my head off at the slightest provocation ever since she and Michael had split.

'Oh, wow!' Sean exclaimed after Mum had taken us in through the front door and he had gone to have a look in one of the reception rooms.

Mum and I went to see what he was wowing about. We found him gazing out of the window at the massive back garden, which was full of cherry blossom trees.

'Oh!' I gasped as I took in the mass of colour – pinks and pale purples and creams. It made me smile just looking at it, and I glanced at Mum, hoping it might cheer her up a little too.

Mum didn't even seem to see the blossom. Her face still wore the same frozen-over expression as she said, 'Well, it's not *this* window that's open. Come on. Let's check the others. God, it's depressing in here.'

I looked at Sean, not bothering to hide my astonishment.

'Depressing?' I murmured, because to me it felt like a house from a story, somewhere something magical could happen. The fireplace had a beautiful carved wood surround and gorgeous ceramic tiles depicting pink birds on a green and gold leafy background. Normally Mum would have been in raptures over that – and over the original wooden floor.

As far back as I can remember, Mum has always talked about her dream house. Now it's like this game we all play. Mum wants big windows and high ceilings, open fires, at least two proper bathrooms and a lovely big garden. And she thinks the Victorian and Edwardian houses have the most character. She thinks *our* house is poky and box-like with no character whatsoever, and it's true, I suppose. Our house is certainly much smaller than Lily's and we don't even have a proper garden, just a small rectangle of lawn and a little patio. Sean and I used to share a bedroom until a couple of years ago, when Mum decided we were too old. We had to draw straws to see who'd keep the room we were in and I lost. I had to move into what had until then been the box room, where Mum kept her work stuff and lots of Dad's old things. Sean kept our big bedroom all to himself, with a desk and book-shelves where my bed used to be. Mum tried to make my new bedroom look nice – I've got a platform bed with a desk underneath, and we painted the walls pale blue and stuck a big mirror on one wall to make it feel bigger. But you can't really fit two people in there, which is why I always end up going round to Lily's place now that we're older. Perhaps that's why Blossom House means so much to me. It totally makes up for my lack of space at home.

'That floor could be so beautiful if it was polished up a bit, couldn't it, Mum?' I said, running after her. 'Maybe *we* could polish it up. We could polish up *all* the floors if you like. It might help you sell the house.'

'It's not our job to polish the floors,' Mum snapped as she went around checking the other downstairs windows. 'Anyway, that sort of thing doesn't make any difference when a house is this overpriced. Frankly, I don't think the old lady's son is ready to sell his childhood home at all. If he wasn't a friend of Miranda's, I doubt we'd be wasting our time having it on the market at this price, but Miranda thinks we might get him to see sense in the end and she doesn't want to miss out.'

'Why doesn't he come back and live here himself if he loves it that much?' I asked. 'He could totally do it up and make it really beautiful again!' (Mum and I are both big fans of all those home improvement programmes on TV, where you see them doing up all sorts of neglected houses.)

28

'He's been living in Canada for a good ten years now, according to Miranda. Came back for his mother's funeral and to sort out the house and put it on the market. Miranda says he needs to sell it but he's just not quite ready to let it go.'

I followed Mum up the wide Victorian staircase with its beautiful carved wooden banister rail, and we found the open window on the landing. There was a lovely oak window seat and I thought how, if I lived here, I'd have scatter cushions on the seat and sit there whenever I wanted to have some quiet time all on my own. I imagined myself as a Victorian girl in a beautiful long dress sitting in the window seat, doing embroidery, or wearing an even grander gown of the finest silk and lace, sweeping down the staircase towards the ballroom where all my guests awaited me.

Normally Mum lets me look around with her if a house is empty and we don't have anywhere else we have to be, but that day when I asked her she said that she just wanted to go straight home.

And when we got home she went upstairs to her bedroom, where she closed the curtains and lay on the bed with the radio turned up loud so we wouldn't hear her crying about Married Michael.

Mum had elected not to get up at all the following morning and I was really taken aback when Sean announced that he had a surprise for me. It turned out he had 'borrowed' Mum's set of keys to Blossom House. 'Let's go back and take a proper look inside without Mum,' he suggested.

'Oh, Sean, I don't think –'

'It'll be fun and we're not doing any harm. Come on. It's better than having to stay in the same house with Mum at the moment. Every time I come home I feel like somebody just died.'

Sean was right – being at home with Mum *was* pretty depressing.

'What if someone finds out?'

'Even if they do, I don't reckon anyone will care. The guy who owns it is in another country, Miranda never goes there and Mum doesn't care about anything right now except Michael.' He grinned as he added, 'Come on, Sasha. Blossom House is lonely and unwanted. Who better than you and me to give it some love?'

I know that we were only ten then, and you wouldn't normally expect two ten-year-olds to go and explore an empty house all by themselves, but back then Sean and I did a lot of stuff without Mum and had already learned to be quite independent. Sometimes Mum was so tired she forgot about dinner, so Sean and I got quite good at making beans on toast or scrambled eggs, or else we'd take Mum's purse and go round the corner to pick up chips for all of us. Our primary school was really close, which meant we could get there and back by ourselves quite easily. So going to Blossom House without Mum didn't feel that weird.

And it wasn't as if she noticed when we kept going back.

Over time I had swept and polished up all the wooden floors and cleaned some of the windows. Last summer I'd got some cushions from the charity shop and made a cosy nook in the window seat. Afterwards, the big main room looked particularly beautiful whenever the sun shone in through the huge sash windows – not that Mum ever noticed on her brief visits to check up on the place.

Now Blossom House sort of felt as if it belonged to us.

'I'm coming with you,' I told Sean firmly. We hadn't been since we'd got back from Greece and maybe the cherry blossom would be out by now. In any case, I didn't see why he should be the only one to get to check up on the place.

Sean just grunted in reply. Frankly, I was starting to feel pretty annoyed with him. I absolutely hate it when he shuts me out like this. When we were younger we'd told each other everything and been pretty much insep-arable. It was only after the move to secondary school that things started to change between us.

He turned towards me suddenly, looking unusually serious. 'Listen, I've got something to tell you that you're not gonna like . . .'

'Are you OK?' I asked. 'You're not in trouble at school, are you? Are you worried about going back?' In the past I'd always have known when he was in trouble without having to ask.

'It's nothing like that. I've arranged to meet Zack at Blossom House,' he said.

I just stared at him. Zack, his new best buddy, was generally viewed as a bit of a weirdo. The main attraction for Sean, as far as I could tell, was that Zack kept lots of weird reptiles and creepy-crawlies as pets.

'You told Zack?' I finally got out.

'Zack has got something he needs to keep secret and I said he could keep it at Blossom House,' Sean told me.

'What is it?' I demanded. 'And what about keeping *Blossom House* a secret?'

'Don't worry, Sasha. Zack won't tell anyone about Blossom House,' he assured me, ignoring the first part of my question. 'Look, I'm a bit late so I'm going to run. I'll see you there.' He glanced down at my feet as he spoke. He had seen me trying to run in my flip-flops while we were in Greece and he knew there was no way I'd be able to keep up.

I felt anger boiling inside me as he tore off ahead of me along the pavement. Sean and I had both sworn a solemn oath not to tell *anyone* about Blossom House, not even our best friends. I hadn't even mentioned the place to Lily.

I thought back to the beginning when the two of us had first started hanging out there, letting ourselves in and out with our own keys. I'd known that what we were doing was wrong, but I'd let my brother persuade me that we were acting as house-sitters, protecting the house from squatters and the like.

For ages we visited the house once or twice a week, mainly at the weekends but sometimes after school too. In the summer holidays we'd bring little picnics with us and I'd read a book on a rug in the garden while Sean lazed on the grass doing stuff on his phone. Sometimes I'd go there on my own – especially after Lily and I had argued, or when Mum or Granny were driving me mad.

We've always had to be careful not to put on any lights after dark or do anything else which might alert the neighbours, but because Blossom House is detached, with trees and a thick hedge on either side, and with a back garden that isn't overlooked, we've always felt pretty safe. And though we had to be prepared for unexpected house viewings, there were hardly any, and as time went by Blossom House began to feel more and more like our very own private hideaway.

We had escaped to it a lot, right up until recently, when our own home had become a much cheerier place to be again. We'd stopped hanging out at Blossom House quite so often, but it had still remained our own special secret.

Until now . . .

Chapter Four

When I eventually reached the house I stopped briefly to admire the magnolia tree, its branches heavy with blossom. There was no sign of Sean or Zack so I hurried down the weedy gravel drive, past the front porch with its sandstone pillars and round to the tall wooden side gate, which my brother had left unlocked. I walked right past the sign saying 'Trespassers will be prosecuted'. I'd never thought that meant Sean and me.

When I reached the back garden I couldn't stop myself breaking into a massive smile. The cherry blossom trees were in full bloom and for a moment all I could focus on was the mass of beautiful pastel-coloured petals. Mum says that even as a baby I always loved flowers, and that my dad was always taking pictures of me holding them or smelling them or sitting in a field full of them. And sometimes when I see beautiful flowers or blossoming trees I get this silly dreamy notion that my dad is looking down on me from heaven, or wherever he is, and smiling along with me.

I looked at the house and my smile faded as I saw my brother and Zack through the window of the downstairs back room. They were looking at something on the floor.

I had a bad feeling as I opened the back door. I kept thinking of how Sean's eyes would light up with excitement as he described how Zack's pet tarantula, Tallulah, had a very hairy bottom to sense any predators that were sneaking up behind her. Or how cool it was feeding live crickets to Zack's two lizards, Tex and Mex. Or how awesome it was to watch Zack's corn snake, Percy, swallowing his weekly meal of a dead mouse. Sean and Zack had actually filmed Percy swallowing a mouse (head first) and added a soundtrack of spaghetti-sucking noises when Percy got to the tail. They'd posted it on YouTube and they were always checking to see how many hits they'd got. (Really, twelve-year-old boys are totally gross.)

I burst into the back reception room.

They were both squatting on the floor next to a large plastic box. That's when my worst fears were confirmed. Well, not my worst, because that would have been the tarantula, but when I saw the snake on the floor in front of them, I let out a loud and very genuine scream.

Sean looked cross. 'Shut up, Sasha. You'll scare him.'

'*Me* scare *him*?' I took a wobbly step backwards.

'It's OK, Sasha, he's not dangerous,' Zack said at once.

'Is that what I think it is?' I pointed to the snake, which had a suspicious-looking lump a short way down its long body.

'Yeah,' Sean said. 'We just fed him.'

'That's disgusting,' I snapped.

'No, it's not,' Zack said, quickly defending his pet. 'It's perfectly natural. *You* eat dead animals, don't you?'

Before I could reply, Sean said with a stupid laugh, 'Not *whole* ones, she doesn't. You know . . . with the skin, and the eyes and the ears, and the cute little hands and feet and tail.'

'Shut up, Sean,' I hissed at him.

Zack didn't look fazed. 'The point is she still eats them.' He looked gravely at me. 'And in any case, *you* have a choice about what to eat, Sasha, because you're an omnivore. Monty *isn't*.'

'Monty?' I was keeping my gaze fixed steadily on the snake, which had quite attractive gold, brown and black patterned scales. 'I thought he was called Percy. He's a corn snake, right?' Mum and I had already looked up 'corn snake' on the internet just to satisfy ourselves that they were as harmless as my brother claimed.

'*Percy* is a corn snake,' Zack said. 'But this isn't Percy. This is Monty and he's a ball python.'

'A *python*!' I only just stopped myself from screaming again. 'Oh my God! Isn't that poisonous?'

'You mean *venomous* and no . . . he isn't,' Zack replied calmly. 'Pythons are constrictor snakes.'

'You mean the kind who coil round you and *squeeze* you to death? Oh my God!' I had stepped right back to stand outside the room now.

'Oh, quit being so dramatic, Sasha,' Sean said abruptly. 'He's way too small to constrict *you*!' He actually stroked the snake as he added, 'Don't let her get to you, Monty – you just keep chomping away.'

'*Digesting* away,' Zack corrected him. 'He doesn't have teeth, remember.'

'Sorry, professor,' Sean said, as it thankfully clicked with me that the snake's mouth probably *was* quite small compared with the size of a human head.

'Monty isn't mine,' Zack told me. 'This guy I know wanted to get rid of him so I said I'd take him, but when I asked Mum and Dad they said no. Mum read something about how a huge python in Africa swallowed a child in some village or something. I keep telling her that Monty is too small to swallow a child but she won't listen. Plus she's worried about my sister's new kitten . . .'

Before I could speak, Sean said, 'So I told him we could keep Monty here. It'll be cool, Sasha. Mum's way too scared of snakes to ever let me have one at home. I reckon this'll be the next best thing.'

'Are you *crazy*? What if Mum has to show someone round?'

'We'll hide him.'

'Where?' I demanded. Zack was already placing the snake back inside its container on top of a towel with something rubbery poking out from under it. 'Is that a hot-water bottle?'

'That's right,' Zack replied. 'Snakes like to be kept warm. But the hot-water bottle's just to keep him comfy while we transport him. When we get him upstairs I'm going to plug in his heat mat. There is somewhere to plug it into, right?'

'Don't worry,' Sean said. 'This cupboard I told you about has a plug socket just outside. We can plug it into that and run the cable under the door. Come on. Let's take him upstairs.'

'It shouldn't take me too long to find him a permanent home,' Zack said. 'You never know. I might be able to talk my mum round.'

'Listen, I really don't think this is a good idea,' I exclaimed as I followed them up the staircase.

I knew where we were going. There was a huge walk-in cupboard in the main front bedroom on the first floor and one rainy day, when Sean and I had been exploring the house, we'd discovered three old dresses and a stack of old board games inside. There had been a few bits and pieces like that left behind in various places around the house and I was guessing they were things that the old lady's son hadn't wanted but hadn't quite had the heart to get rid of either.

'It'll be OK, Sasha. Stop worrying so much,' Sean said impatiently as he opened the cupboard for Zack.

Zack obviously spotted the board games straight away because he read out, 'Tiddlywinks ... Ludo ... Beetle ... *Snakes and Ladders* ...' He added with a laugh, 'Well, Monty, I reckon that's the one to go for if you get bored.'

I waited while they lifted up the snake and took out the hot-water bottle and towel, leaving only a thin layer of newspaper on the bottom of the container for Monty

40

to lie on. Then Zack produced a small heat mat out of his bag and plugged it in.

'Isn't that dangerous?' I queried. 'I mean, what if it starts a fire or something?'

'That's why there's the thermostat with it,' Zack said as he plugged that in too and showed us how it worked. 'Now it can't overheat . . . the heat mat goes *under* the box, like this,' he added as he showed us how to position the mat with the container half on and half off it.

'Don't worry, Monty, you're going to be fine with Uncle Sean and Auntie Sasha,' Sean joked as he went to fill up a big bowl of water to put in the container.

'Watch out for those dresses – they're really old and delicate,' I warned Zack as he disappeared inside the cupboard, carrying Monty's bulky box.

I was pretty sure the dresses we had discovered along with the games dated back to the 1950s. I'd looked them up and in the 1950s all the women had beautifully styled hair and wore masses of lipstick, and even when they were really young they looked so glamorous, like film stars, and they all had ever so tiny waists. The old lady must have been very small and slight when she had worn the dresses, because they actually fitted me – though on me the skirts were more ankle length than calf length. One dress was made of emerald green satin with a stiff bodice and a softly pleated, three-layered swishy skirt trimmed with green ribbon. Another had a fitted black velvet bodice and a fuchsia-pink silk skirt, covered with a fine layer of black netting that was studded with tiny black gems. But my favourite of the three was a halter neck red taffeta dress, which had a fitted bodice decorated with red sparkly beads and a very full floaty skirt.

'Monty should be fine in here for a while,' Zack told my brother as he came back with the water. 'It's nice and warm and he won't need to be fed for another week. But watch you leave those air holes uncovered.' He made a big thing of sliding the three dresses along the rail away from Monty's box as if he was afraid they might slip off their hangers and cut off Monty's air supply.

As Zack came out of the cupboard I said anxiously, 'Listen, Zack, you *have* to leave now. And you have to swear not to tell *anyone* you came here. Do you promise?'

Zack gave me an exasperated look. 'Sasha, just chill, OK? Of course I won't tell anyone. It's *your* friends you need to worry about. If Lily and her pals ever find out about this –'

'They won't,' I snapped, practically pushing him ahead of me down the stairs to send him on his way. 'Just *go*, will you?'

After Zack had left – checking his watch and swearing when he saw the time because apparently his parents were really strict about him being home at whatever time they said – I turned and yelled my brother's name. I was ready to murder him. How *could* he bring Zack here without even asking me? This was where we came when Mum was moody or we needed to escape. It was the only place where Sean and I really talked together like we used to. And to actually let Zack bring that snake . . .

Chapter Five

Sean and I were walking back to our house in icy silence, when I spotted Lily in the distance.

She was walking towards us with Clara and Hanna, two of the popular girls in our year who she hangs out with. Needless to say they are both super confident and good-looking. Clara is tall with short dark hair and she's already pretty busty. After school she always hikes up her skirt to well above her knees to show off her super-long legs. Hanna is shorter and slimmer with a mop of bushy red hair, and the only reason she doesn't do the same with her skirt is because she's scared her mum will find out. I prefer Hanna to Clara, but to be honest both of them make me feel like some sort of social misfit.

I knew Hanna had just spent her Easter holiday in Poland with her grandparents, leaving Clara and Lily to hang out together at home. Which was a pity because Clara is my least favourite of all Lily's friends and now she had her arm around Lily's shoulder as if she owned her.

'There's Leo's car,' Sean said as we approached our house. 'Mum said he was bringing pizza. I hope he's remembered extra pepperoni on mine.'

Just then Lily saw us and waved. I waved back.

'You're honoured today, Sasha,' Sean teased. 'Looks like the A-list might be going to pay you a visit.'

'Shut up, Sean.'

I had a sudden horrible thought that maybe Lily had told the others about Mum and Leo getting engaged. But I told myself to stop being stupid. Lily likes a good gossip, so you have to make it clear when something you tell her is a secret, but if she promises not to tell, then she never does. At least she never has so far.

I saw Lily glance at Leo's car. I knew that she knew it was his. Did the other two? Mum was always reminding Sean and me that if anyone spotted Leo at our house I was to say that he and Mum were friends and that we knew Leo because he'd been Sean's tutor.

I stopped to readjust my flip-flop while I waited for them to reach me. If we had to have a chat, then I didn't want it to be right outside my front door. Sean had already gone on ahead.

I really hoped Lily wasn't about to embarrass me in front of her friends. Not that she'd do that on purpose. It's just that Lily isn't always very subtle in the way she goes about things. I know she *means* well when she tries to demonstrate to her other friends that I'm not actually as dorky as they think, but she usually just makes things worse.

'Hi,' I said, standing up straight as the threesome approached. 'What are you lot doing here?'

Oops! I'd been aiming for super-casual but it had clearly come out kind of aggressive, judging by the way Lily frowned at me.

'Don't worry – we're not calling in for *you*, Sasha,' Clara replied sharply.

'The girls called round for me just after you left,' Lily told me quickly. 'We're on our way to Ellie's house. Did you know she lives at the other end of your street?'

I shook my head. Ellie is new to Helensfield High. She joined midway through the previous term and I don't really know her since I'm not in any of her classes.

'Ellie's mum's a beautician,' Hanna informed me. 'Isn't that cool?'

'Sure,' I said. One of Mum's friends was a beautician and had promised to help if I had trouble with my skin when I hit my teens. 'It's handy knowing a beautician,' I continued, trying my best to have the sort of conversation I thought Lily wanted. 'Especially when you have bad skin.'

The three of them just stared at me.

'Oh . . . no . . . I didn't mean any of *you* have bad skin. I just meant . . .' I trailed off as Clara self-consciously touched a spot on her chin and gave me a glare before stalking off with Hanna. Not that they stalked very far when they saw Lily wasn't following.

Lily snapped, 'Sasha what is *wrong* with you? Why do you have to sound so snotty?'

'Sorry . . . it just came out wrong,' I whispered. 'They make me nervous . . .' I'm pretty sure Lily's new friends don't rate me very highly, even though Lily tries to deny it, which is one of the reasons I always avoid hanging out with them. I prefer to stick with the people I feel comfortable with, and who I know like me just the way I am, even if that does make me a bit of a nobody on the social front.

Before I knew it, Lily was reaching into my jeans pocket where she knows I keep my phone, pulling it out and slamming it into my hand. 'You never check your texts either. I sent you one half an hour ago.'

'Sorry . . .' I started to fumble with my phone and saw that she was right about the text. I looked at Lily questioningly after I'd read it. 'A party?'

To be honest I was feeling a bit miffed. How come my best friend had made party plans with Clara and Hanna rather than me?

'We only just decided,' Lily told me as if she could read my mind. 'It was Raffy's idea. I mean, it's his party really.'

'Raffy's?' I felt myself getting a tiny bit more interested when I heard that.

'Yeah, we just found out that Mum and Dad are going away next weekend,' she told me. 'It's just for one night and for the first time ever they're actually going to leave us on our own. Raffy's in charge and Auntie Jo is going to pop in to check up on us. But, basically, we've got the place to ourselves.'

'So it'll be an "empty", you mean?' I couldn't imagine that Lily's mum would give her permission for this. I knew Mum would freak if Sean and I ever held a party like that behind her back when she wasn't at home, and I don't think I'd even want to. Call me boring if you like, but I just can't see the attraction of risking your house getting trashed or the entire Sixth Form turning up, smoking and drinking and refusing to leave.

'It'll be mostly Year Tens,' Lily explained, 'but Raffy says I get to invite some of my friends as well. So . . . do you want to come? I need an answer now so I know how many other people I can invite. Raffy is being very strict about the numbers. He says he doesn't want too many little kids hanging around. I said we're not little kids. But anyway, he says if we have too many people it could get out of hand.'

'That's sensible of him,' I said, thinking that I really hoped Raffy didn't think *I* was a little kid. 'So how many people is he inviting?'

'A hundred.'

'A *hundred*?' I gaped at her.

'Raffy thinks they won't all come and we can't risk not having enough people there,' Lily continued. 'Anyway, *you're* invited.'

'And Sean,' said Hanna, flicking back her wiry red hair as she came back over to join us along with Clara. 'Tell him it's going to be a really cool party.'

'But you can't bring any of your dorky friends from school,' Clara told me. 'And tell Sean not to bring Zack.'

'What's wrong with Zack?' I demanded. (Goodness knows why I was sticking up for *him* all of a sudden.)

'Nothing – apart from the fact he's a total weirdo,' Clara replied.

'Sasha's dorky friends probably wouldn't want to come anyway,' Hanna said matter-of-factly. 'It wouldn't be their scene. I mean, can you imagine Jillian or Priti actually enjoying themselves at our party?'

'That's true,' Clara laughed. 'It'd be way too much fun for them! In fact Jillian would probably bring her chess set.'

The others giggled.

I glared at them all. Jillian and Priti are two of the new friends I've made at Helensfield High. Jillian is super-bright and chess-mad. She's been playing since she was three, and all her chess tournaments keep her very busy outside school. Priti is the new friend I've become really close to. She's clever and quite studious and she's always reading books and writing stuff. She wants to be a professional poet when she grows up. Leo is her English teacher and apparently he's the only one who encourages her to be a poet, though even he says she'll probably have to combine it with another career if she wants to earn a living.

'You'd better be careful, Lily,' I warned her shirtily. 'You don't want your neighbours calling the police, and let's face it, with a hundred people partying in your house, then they're probably going to.'

'Oh . . . stop being such a killjoy, Sasha,' Lily snapped.

'Hey . . . right up until the police arrive I'm sure it'll be a great party,' I added with a smirk.

'Ha. Ha.'

'Remember, Sasha,' Hanna said gravely, 'you have to keep this a *total* secret. Clara and I are telling our parents we're going to Lily's for a sleepover. If you want to come then you'd better tell *your* mum the same thing.'

I glared at Hanna, feeling like telling her to stop being so patronising.

'Oh, Sasha's mum wouldn't rat us out in any case,' Lily informed them swiftly. 'She's more like a really cool big sister than a mum. Do you remember that time she took us with her to that cocktail party, Sasha?' She turned to the other two, adding, 'My mum nearly had a fit when she found out, even though we only drank non-alcoholic cocktails.'

I sighed. It was a story Lily never tired of telling.

'Hey, I like your flip-flops, Sasha!' Hanna suddenly said. 'Did your mum get them for you?'

I glared at her. 'No.'

'Sasha actually has much better taste in clothes and shoes and stuff than you'd think,' Lily told them.

'Lily!' I felt my cheeks flaming and I was about to tell her she could stuff her stupid party, but just in time I stopped myself.

'I'll *try* and make it to your party,' I said frostily. 'If you're sure you wouldn't rather have my *mum* instead?'

'Don't be daft.' Lily was frowning, looking like she might be about to say more.

Before she had the chance I stalked off with my head held high. And if I hadn't tripped on my loose flip-flop five seconds later, I reckon I'd have made a passably cool exit.

Chapter Six

I can't explain why I didn't stand up for Priti and Jillian when Lily and her friends were so rude about them. I felt really disloyal afterwards, but at the time I was just flattered that I was invited to Raffy's party. And after Lily called me a killjoy, I suppose I got a bit preoccupied wondering if she could be right.

Leo and my brother were both in the kitchen when I got inside. There were pizza cartons sitting on the table and the smell immediately set my stomach rumbling.

'Hey, Sasha. How are you doing?' Leo greeted me as he helped himself to a beer from our fridge. He pushed a chunk of dark unruly hair out of his eyes as he straightened up, adding, 'Your mum's had to go into work for a bit. She won't be long but she said for us to go ahead and eat without her.'

'Sasha, look! He actually *remembered* my extra pepperoni,' Sean told me with a grin, opening the lid of the top pizza box and inhaling dramatically.

I didn't say anything. I still felt too angry with Sean to talk to him properly.

Leo went over and whacked the cardboard lid down on top of Sean's fingers. 'Paws off, greedy-guts. Now Sasha's here we can sit at the table and eat in a civilised fashion.'

'Or we could eat in an *un*civilised fashion in front of the telly,' Sean quipped.

Leo laughed as he handed my brother the top pizza carton. Unlike Mum, whose mood tends to go up and down a lot, Leo is almost always cheerful. At least he is at home. At school he can be pretty serious and strict if you start mucking about in his class. Or so I've heard. Luckily, Sean and I aren't in his class for English, though he'd told us on holiday that he was going to be standing in for our registration teacher for a couple of weeks after Easter. That was going to be weird. Even thinking about it made me feel a bit odd.

Just then the phone rang and Leo picked it up, clearly expecting it to be Mum.

Too late, we looked at the caller display. It was Granny.

Leo's eyes narrowed as he listened to whatever our grandmother was saying at the other end. 'Did she? I see . . . Well, sorry, but I'm afraid she's had to pop out . . . Yes, I'll get her to call you . . . Yes . . . OK . . .' Leo was clearly planning to hang up the phone, but Sean snatched it from him.

'Hi, Granny!' he said breezily. 'Mum was phoning you to tell you that she and Leo got engaged on holiday! It's cool, isn't it? Leo's going to be your new son-in-law.'

Leo stood there gaping at him.

A long silence followed, and then Sean said, 'Granny, are you still there?'

Her delayed but extremely loud exclamation of disbelief was audible to all of us. Sean grinned as he reassured Granny that of course he wasn't joking and even offered to hand her over to Leo again to corroborate the news.

Leo shook his head furiously at that idea but he needn't have worried because the only person Granny really wanted to speak to was Mum. Sean told her to try Mum on her mobile and then he listened for a few more minutes, murmuring, 'OK, Granny, see you then,' a couple of times. Finally he hung up, looking very pleased with himself.

'Mum's going to kill you, Sean,' I told him.

'Not if I do it first,' Leo said grimly.

'Look, Mum didn't want to tell Granny, so now I've done the job for her. She's going to thank me,' my brother protested.

'Not after your grandmother's called her at work and given her an earful,' Leo pointed out.

'Mum'll see it's Granny and she won't answer,' Sean said smoothly. 'That's why you *have* caller display, Leo. So you can see who it is *before* you pick up the phone. Oh . . . before I forget, Granny wants to come and visit us this week. I think she wants to make sure you haven't brainwashed Mum into marrying you or anything!'

'This week? *When* this week?' Leo sounded horrified.

'Wednesday or Thursday probably. She's ringing back to let us know.'

Leo pulled such a face that I couldn't help wondering if he was having second thoughts about joining our family.

Mum got home half an hour later and was full of smiles, even though she'd had a conversation with Granny. Leo and Sean and I were watching an action movie with lots of shooting in it. Mum walked straight into the living room, picked up the remote and switched off the TV.

'HEY!' the three of us shouted indignantly.

'You shouldn't be watching such a violent film. It's not good for you.' She sounded just like Granny, though none of us dared tell her that.

'Don't worry, Annie. There were no really gross scenes,' Leo said jokily. 'The blood didn't even look real, did it, kids?'

Mum gave him a *you're-not-funny* sort of look as she turned to us. 'Guess what? It looks like we might have a buyer for Blossom House.'

'No way!' Instantly I felt panicked. I looked at Sean, who was clearly equally horrified.

'Yes. We've got a new client who's actually considering paying the full asking price. Miranda showed him round while we were in Greece apparently.'

'But, Mum, you said nobody would ever be interested in Blossom House while it was so overpriced,' I protested.

Mum was nodding. 'Yes. It's a bit of a surprise, I must say! Miranda thinks he must have more money than sense.'

'But –' I gulped. I didn't know what to say.

'Are you all right, Sasha?' Leo asked.

I quickly put a fake smile on my face and stood up. 'Sure. I'm going upstairs. I want to catch up on my homework before school.'

Sean started to follow – I could tell he was worried now about that stupid snake – but Mum called out sharply from the living room. 'Sean! Come back in here! I want to talk to you!'

'She probably wants to talk about what you said to Granny,' I murmured. He rolled his eyes and turned back.

As I continued upstairs I passed the picture of Grandpa in his magician's costume, then the blown-up photograph of white cherry blossom our dad had taken in the park a few weeks before he died.

I felt my eyes fill up at the thought that we might be about to lose Blossom House after all this time. I forced the tears back down and gave myself a fierce talking to: *Come on, Sasha! It's just a house. No matter how much you love it, it's not like you're losing an actual person . . .*

Chapter Seven

Maybe this is the point where I should tell you a bit about our dad.

Sean and I were five when he collapsed suddenly one afternoon on the floor of our living room. As I watched him being taken away in the ambulance, I don't think I had any actual thoughts at the time about not seeing him ever again. But I do remember a certain feeling that I had – as if something catastrophic was happening or was about to happen.

It had started out as a perfectly ordinary day. Sean and I were playing 'Knights and Princesses' and Sean was rescuing me. At first we didn't notice anything was wrong, then Mum was all panicky, talking and crying on the phone, and rushing us out of the room. An ambulance appeared and we watched our dad being loaded into it on a stretcher. Our neighbour came to look after us while

Mum went with him to the hospital. She fed us lots of biscuits and let us watch TV until really late, and when we woke up the next morning Granny was there and Mum was in her room in bed as if *she* was the one who was ill. Granny had to sit with Mum the whole time until the doctor came and gave her some medicine to help her sleep.

Granny and the doctor sat Sean and me down and told us together that our daddy had died in the night.

I can remember a few bits about the funeral service. I remember thinking our dad might actually be there in some form or another, and being quite disappointed when he wasn't. I think I asked Granny where he was in the church and she pointed to the coffin, but I still didn't really understand what was going on.

Afterwards a lot of people came back to our house and I remember sitting with Sean on the patio, trying to change the direction of an army of ants by feeding them a trail of breadcrumbs. It was a sunny day and people were standing on the grass in black clothes, talking to each other and eating party food.

Some grown-ups we didn't know came over to talk to us, wanting to know what we were doing. They immediately donated some of their strawberry tart to our ant project, advising us that ants especially liked sweet things. Sure enough we soon had that ant army under our control.

'Do you know our daddy?' I remember asking them.

At the mention of our dad, Sean started looking around the garden as if he was trying to spot him. He'd been doing that a lot.

'Daddy's not here,' I reminded him in my most grown-up, talking-to-a-baby sort of voice. 'He's *dead*, remember?'

'I know that, *stupid*!' And he gave me a massive shove and started stamping all over the ants.

Mum thinks that Sean and I were too young to experience proper grief when our dad died. She even thinks it's a blessing we didn't lose him later on, when she reckons it would have hurt us more. But I don't agree with her on that. I wish I could remember him as an actual person a lot better, instead of just being left with some faint and disjointed memories and that achy feeling of *wanting him* that I can remember as clearly as anything.

Mum seemed to cry all the time after he died and sometimes it felt like she was never going to stop. Granny gave up trying to distract her in the end, and basically left her to it when she was crying, concentrating on looking after Sean and me instead.

Mum says her heart broke that day and I'm sure it was true because for a long time it was as if she'd just sort of ground to a halt. Sometimes she wanted to be left alone. Other times she couldn't bear to be on her own, not even to sleep, and we'd all go to sleep together, me, Sean and Mum, in her big bed. Lily's mum used to come in the mornings to take us to school, and on really bad days Mum wouldn't even be up and she'd tell Sean and me not to bother answering the door. Granny came over every day to check up on us (she still lived in the same town as us then) and after a while she ended up moving in with us. She told Sean and me we had to be very grown up and help her look after Mum.

At home I tried to be as grown up and helpful as possible but at school all I wanted to do was draw pictures. I drew lots of different pictures of heaven, all with blue skies, beaches, flowers, bright sunshine, with my dad standing in the middle with his sunhat on and his camera round his neck and a big smile on his face. I drew him a little house to live in and a dog, because I knew he'd always wanted one.

I remember Sean and I went to see a lady who was especially interested in our drawings and the same lady helped Sean and me write goodbye messages to our dad on little coloured labels, which we tied to red balloons and let go of one windy day, watching and waving until they were tiny red dots in the sky. I wrote 'GOODBYE, DADDY, I LOVE YOU' on mine, though I had to get some help with the spelling. Sean wasn't very good at writing so he drew a picture of Dad and him holding hands.

When we were a bit older it was Granny who explained why our dad had died that day. We already knew that it had started with a headache that was so bad it had made him fall on to the floor. I always got worried whenever Mum had a headache and once, when she had a really bad one, I started to cry. That was what prompted Granny to talk to us and she pointed out that mostly when you have a headache it *doesn't* mean you're about to die. Our dad's headache wasn't anything like a normal one, she said. It had happened because a faulty blood vessel in his brain had suddenly burst and caused too much brain damage for his brain to carry on working. It was an extremely rare thing to have a faulty blood vessel in your brain, she said, and we didn't have to worry about it happening to Mum or to us because our blood vessels were all perfectly healthy. And as usual she had said it so firmly and with such certainty that I had been instantly reassured.

It's been seven years now since our dad died and I honestly can't remember him very well at all. I have hazy memories of sitting on his lap while he read me a story, and of playing ball in the park with him and Sean. But I can't remember his face very clearly, or what his voice sounded like.

I do have one very precious memory of him though. He'd taken me outside to see a spider's web glistening in the early morning dew and I remember being both terrified and mesmerised as we watched that big spider dangling by a silver thread right in front of our noses. I remember giggling as he took a photograph of me standing as close to the web and its hairy occupant as I dared. And even now, especially on a frosty morning, I can still remember the thrill of being there with him that day, just the two of us in our yet-to-be-shattered world.

Chapter Eight

Monday was our first day back at school after the Easter break. I rolled my eyes at my brother when I came downstairs and saw him trying to scrape off a bit of breakfast from his school tie. At least the rest of his clothes – dark grey trousers, white school shirt and grey V-necked jumper with our school logo on it – still looked freshly washed and ironed though I knew they wouldn't stay that way for long. Sean looks a lot younger in his school uniform, though I know better than to tell him that.

Helensfield High has a very strict uniform policy – even Leo says that whoever wrote it was clearly a bit obsessional. The rules include wearing your tie with 'at least three double stripes visible below a small neat knot' and wearing skirts of a length 'no more than two inches above the knee'. Wearing make-up is a total no-no, though I once wore some of Mum's mascara to school to test out

Lily's theory that my eyelashes are so short that mascara only makes them look normal. (And unfortunately it turned out she was right, because nobody noticed.)

Lily, Clara and Hanna came up to talk to me the second I walked into the playground.

'Sasha, we've all been talking,' Lily began, 'and we really want you to hang out with *us* today.'

'You do?' I'm ashamed to say that I actually felt quite flattered. Right up until they started their recruitment spiel, that is.

'Yes,' Hanna said. 'Because Lily's got a point about how you shouldn't judge a book by its cover.'

'Its cover?'

'Yeah.' Lily explained hastily, 'I was telling them how you might not *look* as if you'd fit into our group, Sasha, but how all that surface stuff isn't what's important. I mean, you're pretty cool on the *inside*. That's what I keep saying.'

'Not that it wouldn't be fun to do one of those total makeover things on you,' Clara added.

'Pardon?'

'Nobody's saying you need a makeover, Sasha,' Lily said as she glared at Clara.

'Not unless you want one,' Hanna put in – which made Lily glare at her too.

Out of the corner of my eye I could see Priti waiting for me on the other side of the playground. I decided it was time to join her, but before I could, Raffy suddenly appeared beside us. 'Lily . . . Dad phoned home after you left for school. They've got to cancel their weekend away. Dad's got to work.'

'Oh no!'

'We need to tell everybody we invited to the party. If anyone turns up on Saturday night, we're dead.'

Lily, Hanna and Clara all started talking at once.

'Hi, Raffy,' I greeted him shyly as he turned to go back to his friends.

Raffy glanced briefly at me and then, to my horror, his gaze shifted down to my totally unflattering school shoes.

'They're my granny's,' I blurted out stupidly, just in case he thought they were my own choice.

'You're wearing your granny's shoes?' He was grinning, looking at me like I was a complete idiot.

'My granny's *choice*, I mean . . . not her actual shoes . . .' I was blushing furiously. 'She took me shopping and . . .' I only just stopped myself from launching into the whole sorry story where the shop assistant had told Granny that these ones provided the best support for growing feet and Granny had flatly refused to let me have any others. Honestly, what was wrong with me? I shouldn't feel like I had to justify my shoes to Lily's brother.

'Catch you later, Sasha.' Raffy gave me a big smile, almost as if he didn't think I was the dorkiest girl in the playground.

I watched him return to his friends. I felt a bit weak at the knees as he strode away from me, his blazer flung ever so casually over one shoulder. I thought he could easily be a model in a TV advert for school uniforms or something.

I left Lily and her friends to sort out their party drama and hurried over to join Priti.

'I saw you ogling Rafferty just now,' she teased, putting away the Jane Austen novel she'd been reading.

'I was not,' I protested.

'Then why have you just gone bright red?'

Priti was giving me a funny look, which made me go even redder, and I quickly turned my face away.

'It's OK, I won't tell anyone. I promise,' she said, still grinning. 'Hey, Mum's going to make samosas again when you come over on Friday since you raved about them so much last time.'

'Cool.' Priti's mum is a brilliant cook.

'She wants to know which kind you liked best. It was the veggie ones, right?'

'Yes,' I agreed, 'but she doesn't have to make them especially for me.'

'Don't be silly. Mum loves cooking for my friends.'

'Wish I could say the same for mine,' I joked, trying not to cringe as I remembered the last time Priti had come for tea. Mum had sent Sean out to buy fish and chips after making a big thing of enquiring if Hindus ate fish and gushing on about how interested she had always been in other cultures and religions. Afterwards I'd told Mum she'd sounded over the top and insincere and that she had embarrassed me, and Mum had told me I was over-thinking the whole thing as usual, and that she had just been trying to make Priti feel welcome.

As the bell rang I told Priti about Lily's party and how it wasn't going ahead after all.

'Good,' she murmured.

I gave her a sharp look.

'Well, you were going to get caught for sure. You would have got into loads of trouble. Lily was stupid to think she could invite all those people and get away with it.'

I sighed. She was right, I guess. But I suspected the real reason Priti was so unsympathetic was because she hadn't been invited to the party herself.

The rest of the day at school was pretty uneventful. It wasn't until we were leaving at half past three that I spotted my brother standing with Leo in the playground. That was unusual, since they generally tended to avoid each other in school.

Then I realised Sean was getting told off – not that it seemed to be having much effect on him. He had his tie wrapped around his head like it was fancy dress and his mates were sloping off.

'Chill, Leo, your boss isn't even in school today, remember,' I heard Sean say cheekily as I approached them. Our gruff Scottish headmaster was away.

'Which is why I'm the one speaking to you about this and not him!' Leo snapped. 'Now get that tie off your head and back round your neck before I'm tempted to strangle you with it!'

'Yeah, yeah, don't get your trunks in a twist,' Sean said. I couldn't believe he was talking to Leo like that at school.

'Listen, Sean, I suggest you think hard about your attitude,' Leo said calmly. 'I'll talk to you later.'

He broke off abruptly when Lily appeared alongside us.

My stomach just about dropped to the floor as she smiled knowingly at Leo and said, 'Hello, Mr Anderson. Did you have a good Easter holiday?'

Leo delayed just a couple of seconds more than usual before answering, 'I did, thank you, Lily. What about you?'

'It was fine, though I missed Sasha.'

'Lily, come on,' I hissed, grabbing her by the arm and pulling her away from them before this whole conversation in the middle of the school playground could get any more embarrassing.

I glanced back to see my brother putting his tie back on while Leo stood watching him.

'Hey, you'll never guess what I heard today,' Lily said as we walked out of school. 'Guess who fancies you, Sasha!'

I instantly felt my cheeks flame. Oh my God! Surely she couldn't mean . . . ?

'Zack!' she declared with a huge grin.

I gaped at her. She had to be kidding me, right?

'Cross my heart,' she continued when she saw the disbelief on my face. 'I mean, I was shocked too. *I* thought Zack was only into reptiles and creepy-crawlies, but apparently he really likes you too.'

'Come off it, Lily! That's rubbish! He's best friends with Sean, and Sean's never mentioned it.'

'Well, it's true! One of Raffy's mates' sisters is friends with Zack's sister and she told me. I can get Raffy to find out for sure if you like.'

'No way!' I said fiercely. 'Don't you *dare* say anything to Raffy. I *mean* it, Lily!'

She held up her hands defensively. 'OK, OK . . . But I thought you *liked* Zack. I mean, you were very quick to defend him when I said I didn't want him at my party. You could've invited him if you'd really wanted to, by the way. I'd just have explained it to the others.'

'Lily, shut up!' I almost yelled at her. 'I don't fancy Zack, OK? And don't you *dare* tell any of the others!'

She was grinning. 'OK, OK . . . keep your hair on! We'll just have to find you a boy who you *do* like . . .'

I gave her a little shove. 'Oh yeah? Well, what about you? Maybe you should find a *real* boy to fancy for a change! One who doesn't sing in a band!'

'Hey, the boys in those bands are real people too! I bet they could do with going out with someone like me. I could help them keep their feet on the ground.'

I laughed. 'Lily, you're the *last* person to keep anybody's feet on the ground!'

'Hey!' She shoved me back, laughing too, and I suddenly had a flashback to when we had first started infant school together. We'd had a very passionate love–hate sort of friendship back then, where we were always falling out and making up again. Lily had become much gentler with me after my dad died. Or maybe it was just that after that a lot of the fight had gone out of me and it suited me to trot around after Lily, doing whatever she said and letting her protect me from everyone and everything.

'You know what my mum said the other day?' Lily said with a giggle. 'That she sometimes wishes she could go back to the time when I had pictures of ponies all over my bedroom. How icky is that?'

I laughed. 'Remember when I had all those posters of kittens?'

Lily nodded. 'That one of the kitten in the deckchair was really cute.' She was smiling as she slipped her arm through mine. 'I'm sure I've still got those pony posters in a bag up in the loft somewhere. We should totally get them down and have a look at them sometime . . .'

Chapter Nine

If anyone was going to tell me that they wished I still had kitten posters in my bedroom it would be Granny rather than Mum. Granny has always played a big part in our lives, so I guess I should tell you a bit more about her before I go any further.

Granny has been like a second mum to Sean and me ever since our dad died. She's very different to Mum in that she's always said that children should be allowed to be children, and I know she tried her best to protect us from having to grow up too fast. When she lived with us she was very hot on bedtimes and table manners and checking up on our day at school. At the same time she'd nag Mum to eat properly, take her medication regularly, keep her doctor's appointments and get enough exercise. Mum argued with her sometimes, saying that she wasn't a child and she didn't want to be treated like one. Granny just ignored that and carried on running our little family the way she wanted it done rather than the way Mum did.

The only trouble with Granny is that she never wants to listen to anybody who disagrees with her. I think she genuinely believes she is always right and therefore far better qualified than everybody else to make most decisions. And I'm fairly sure she honestly thinks she could do a better job of running the country than the prime minister if only she'd chosen to go into politics. Granny *is* a very clever and strong sort of person. She grew up in quite a poor family and got a scholarship to a brilliant school and then became the first person in her family to go to university. And it wasn't just any old university – it was Cambridge. Granny would have had a very successful career after that – as she's fond of telling us – if she hadn't met our grandfather and fallen head over heels in love with him.

Apparently our grandfather had already inherited quite a bit of money from his parents, which had allowed him to follow his dream of becoming a professional magician. When Granny met him, he was travelling all over the country, and even to other countries, doing magic shows. About six months after they met, Granny got pregnant and they got married. She hoped he would settle down and get a more conventional job, or at least give up the travelling so that she could embark on a proper career while he helped look after our mum. But though he made a lot of promises, in the end he never did get any other sort of job. According to Mum, Granny was so ashamed of what he did, she used to tell her friends her husband was a travelling salesman, because she thought it sounded more respectable. And whenever he came home, all Granny wanted to know was when he was going to keep his word and get himself some 'useful employment'. Mum says they argued all the time and her father stayed away from home for longer and longer periods.

I think Mum really loved her dad. She told me she'd longed to travel with him in the holidays, but Granny had never allowed it. Even now Mum's eyes will light up when she describes the mini magic shows he'd put on just for her when she was little – and how he always said she was his favourite audience. He'd magic shiny coins from behind her ears, golden eggs from her school satchel and strings of multicoloured scarves from her pockets. Once on her birthday he'd even produced a real live rabbit from his magician's hat and she had been allowed to keep it as a pet.

Mum has a photograph up in her bedroom of Grandpa and her together, and he certainly looks like he was a fun dad. Mum was ten when that picture was taken and the two of them are standing inside a big dark blue trunk with gold stars painted all over it. The trunk had contained everything her father needed for his magic shows and had travelled everywhere with him. It had gone missing after he died and Mum suspected Granny might have got rid of it without telling her. According to Mum, Granny refused to talk about him after his death and seemed even angrier with him then than she had been when he was alive. 'It was almost as if she thought he'd had that heart attack just to spite her,' Mum told me once.

Anyway, soon Granny would be coming to visit us with the sole purpose of inspecting Leo. I had no doubt she was going to interrogate him thoroughly when they met and I knew Mum wouldn't be able to stop her. Granny would stay for a few days and Mum had decided that she would take us all out to lunch so that the introductions could take place 'on neutral territory'. Plus I think she was hoping that even Granny couldn't make too big a scene so long as we had plenty of witnesses.

Chapter Ten

I'd arranged to meet Sean and Zack at Blossom House after school that day and as I let myself in the back door I can honestly say I didn't feel at all embarrassed about seeing Zack. I mean, there was just no way Lily could be right about him fancying me.

I found my brother sitting on the floor of the upstairs front bedroom with Monty draped over both arms. The snake actually looked quite beautiful with the sun shining on its browny-gold skin.

'Where's Zack?' I asked at once.

'His mum wanted him straight home after school. His auntie is visiting or something.'

'His parents are pretty strict with him, aren't they?' Sean and I had never had a lot of restrictions placed on us by Mum. She said that Granny had been unbearably bossy and over-controlling while *she* was growing up and she was determined not to be like that with us.

'I guess . . .' Sean murmured.

I went to use the bathroom but as I stepped inside I spotted the most enormous spider crawling over the floor.

I screamed. I couldn't help it. It was one of those big dense crusty-looking spiders that seems to expand in size when it starts walking.

My brother rushed in from the bedroom to see what was wrong. 'You're such a wimp,' he said with a grin. Then he told me to go and keep an eye on Monty while he rescued the spider.

I went back into the bedroom, where all I could see was the empty floor. There was no sign of the snake anywhere. 'Sean, where is he?' For a moment I wondered if my brother was playing some kind of prank.

'What?' He left the spider where it was and came back to join me.

'Monty's not here,' I said with a frown.

'He must be here. I left him right in the middle of the floor.' Sean went over to the window and yanked back the curtains to look behind them. But Monty wasn't there either. He also wasn't lying along the curtain rail or, thankfully, dangling down from the lampshade. The cupboard door was closed so he couldn't have gone in there.

Sean went to look under the carpet, which was completely loose at one edge of the room. 'Uh-oh,' he grunted as he pulled it back to reveal rotting green underlay and broken old floorboards with several holes in them big enough for a snake to squeeze through.

'Oh God, Sean . . . what are we going to do?' My mind was already racing ahead, imagining the worst possible scenario as usual . . . a ravenous Monty coming out from under the floorboards while Mum was showing someone round . . . Monty resurfacing in the toilet bowl while somebody was sitting on it . . . Monty's head sticking out of the letterbox to greet the postman in the morning . . .

'Don't panic,' Sean told me, knowing only too well the way my mind works. 'He'll probably reappear in a bit. If he doesn't, we'll call Zack.' Though he sounded worried as he added, 'Trouble is, Zack's always moaning that his mum makes him switch off his phone whenever they're having "family time".'

Suddenly my heart felt like it was beating ten times faster as a brilliant idea came to me. 'I know who we can ask to help.'

And before Sean could reply, I was already taking out my phone to call Lily.

When Lily and I were really little, Raffy had been obsessed with snakes. His parents had never let him have one, but he'd watched loads of nature programmes about them, had adopted a snake at a zoo and had tormented me and Lily with snake stories and videos. You'd never know to look at him now that he'd been such a geek when he was younger.

I'd told Lily that the side gate would be open and that she and Raffy should just knock on the back door when they arrived, but of course, Lily being Lily, she just walked straight in.

'Lily!' I scrambled to my feet from being down on my hands and knees looking for Monty. I'd been searching under the tatty old sofa – the only piece of furniture left in the front room – since the bedroom where we'd been keeping Monty was directly overhead.

'Wow!' Lily exclaimed in admiration as she took in her surroundings. I'd told her about Blossom House over the phone, explaining about the Monty crisis and that we couldn't get hold of Zack and therefore needed Raffy's help.

'Isn't Raffy coming?' I asked.

'I asked him, but he said he doesn't know how to catch a snake and that in any case he's too busy. More like lazy if you ask me. But don't worry. I'll help you look.'

'Oh.' I actually felt a bit let down and it was a struggle not to show it. Luckily, Lily was way too distracted to notice my reaction.

She was walking slowly around the room, staring with wide eyes as if she was in some sort of palace. 'I can't believe you've never told me about this place before! Sasha, you *do* realise this would be the perfect place to hold a party.'

Trust Lily to think of that.

'Yeah, like *that's* really going to happen,' I muttered sarcastically.

'Oh, you're such a scaredy-cat, Sasha!' Lily teased, though I could tell she knew better than to try and push it. 'So where's Sean?'

'Upstairs . . . Lily, you mustn't tell anyone you came here, OK? My mum doesn't even know we come here.' For some reason Zack's warning had suddenly popped back into my head: *If Lily and her pals ever find out about this . . .*

Lily must have picked up on my bout of anxiety because she frowned. 'What's wrong? You sound like you don't trust me.'

'It's not that, it's just –'

'Sasha, have you ever brought Priti here?' she suddenly asked.

'*What?*'

'Well, it feels like maybe you trust *her* more than me!'

'Don't be daft!' I didn't know what else to say. Lily sounded like she was jealous and yet how could she be? Lily is one of the most popular girls in our year. Priti is like . . . well . . . Priti had once joked that if she were a character in a Jane Austen novel she'd be the plain, shy girl standing at the edge of the ballroom while all the beautiful, confident girls were being asked to dance.

'Well, you hang out with her all the time. You know, people at school are starting to think you're going over to the dorky side,' Lily said matter-of-factly.

'I am *not*!' I snapped back indignantly.

'No? Well, sometimes it seems like you're heading that way!' Lily sighed. 'Listen, Sasha, a party here would be so great. Don't you want to do any fun stuff at all?'

'I *do* do fun stuff, Lily!' I protested.

'Like what?' she challenged me. 'You never want to do anything fun with me and the girls. You never come shopping with us or go to the cinema with us or even come down the park with us in the evenings. You only ever hang out with the boring people at school. Priti is bad enough, but that Jillian is seriously uncool. And now your mum is actually getting married to the hottest teacher in our school ... Well, I mean, having Leo in your house could totally get you in with all the popular people ... but you won't even let me *tell* anybody! It's like you *want* to sink into the background!'

I gaped at her. Where had all this come from? I knew she was miffed that I didn't try harder to fit in with the popular crowd she hangs out with, but it wasn't like I went out of my way to embarrass her, or like I minded if she hung out in a different group to me. Why did it have to be such a big deal all of a sudden?

'Don't look at me like that, Sasha! I'm saying this for your own good. The fact is you need to be more image conscious.' She frowned. 'Listen, I know Clara and Hanna can be a bit of a pain, but they're only like that because they think *you* don't rate *them*. If you start hanging out with us a bit more, they'll be fine. And I'm not saying you have to *totally* stop being friends with Priti, but –'

'*You* can't tell me who to be friends with, Lily,' I protested hotly.

'I'm *not* telling you!'

'Yes, you are!'

That was when Sean came into the room and snapped at both of us. 'HEY! I thought you were trying to find Monty!' And he gave Lily a very unsurprised sort of look as he added, 'I guess Raffy's got better things to do, right?'

The three of us searched the house for ages, targeting every nook and cranny we could find. Lily and I barely spoke, but I was glad that she'd still stuck around to help out. I almost asked her why she bothered hanging out with me if she thought I was so boring and dorky, but I stopped myself because I was a bit afraid of the answer. Maybe she was right to complain. Maybe I *was* cramping her style. After all, she'd invited me to a Year Ten party, whereas I'd invited her round to an empty house to search for a runaway snake!

Despite our combined efforts, there was still no sign of Monty.

Lily didn't look me in the eye when she said goodbye. I watched her walk away, then went back to help Sean lock up.

'I guess there's no point in leaving this switched on,' I said as I unplugged Monty's heat mat and pushed the whole box inside the cupboard while Sean looked on miserably.

We left the cupboard door open a little way, just in case he decided to return there while we were gone.

'I'll have to tell Zack,' Sean murmured. 'I'll go round there tonight.'

'Why not just tell him tomorrow? I mean, if they've got family visiting –'

'I'd rather get it over with.'

We had just locked the side gate and we were on our way out of the drive when Mum suddenly appeared from the street.

I nearly had a heart attack on the spot, and by the look of it so did Mum.

'What are you two doing here?' she hissed.

That's when we saw that a well-dressed middle-aged couple were following in her wake, clutching the estate agents' details for Blossom House. Mum hadn't mentioned any more house showings this week. (The potential buyer Miranda had found had gone away on business and wasn't due back for a fortnight.)

'Oh, hi, Mum. We were ﹈
um . . . checking the side gate wa﹈
It was amazing how quickly I could ﹈
protecting our second home. I could te﹈
completely believe my explanation, but fortu﹈
attention was quickly diverted.

Sean was pointing at the sales brochure Mum's clients were holding. 'You know, *I* took a lot of the photos in there,' he informed them proudly. 'Personally, I think they make the place look much bigger and a good bit lighter inside than it really is. And of course they don't show all the damp and the woodworm and the dry rot and stuff like that.' As he started to walk off, he added casually, 'She *has* told you the house is way overpriced, right?'

Poor Mum let out a sort of choking noise and as we scurried away we could hear her apologising profusely for her son's 'extremely dark' sense of humour.

Chapter Eleven

We found Leo's car parked outside our house when we got back. Sean gave a little huff of annoyance, which wasn't like him, but I didn't think much about it until we got inside. We were both on tenterhooks waiting for Mum to ring and tell us Monty had appeared while she was showing round her clients. I couldn't imagine what Mum would do if she saw a snake. Though I suppose she might not blame us for it. I mean, why should she? She might open the cupboard and see the snake box, but there was so much other weird junk still left in Blossom House that hopefully the box alone wouldn't stand out.

'Hi, Leo. Nice smell,' I greeted him. Something garlicky was cooking in the oven.

'Hey, kids. You're late home, aren't you? Where have you been?' Leo asked it lightly, but it was clear he expected an answer from us. That was taking a bit of getting used to. Mum almost never asked us to tell her what we'd been doing after school.

'We've been with Lily,' I answered truthfully.

'Yeah,' Sean grunted. 'And now I'm going round to Zack's. I haven't got time to stop for dinner. I'll get a burger or something. In fact do you have any money and I'll get Mum to pay you back?'

Leo actually laughed.

Sean scowled. 'OK, so I'll buy a bag of chips. I've got enough money for that.'

'Sean, I've already got something in the oven for dinner,' Leo said, beginning to sound irritated. 'Your mum's going to be late so we'll go ahead and eat without her. Anyway, we need to talk about your behaviour at school today. And what about your homework?'

'I haven't got that much.'

'Really? Well, I've heard that you've got a geography assignment still outstanding from the end of last term.'

Sean instantly looked sulky. 'You've heard a lot.'

'Yeah, well . . . teachers talk. And since Rob Mann happens to be a mate of mine as well as your geography teacher . . .'

Sean looked even sulkier. 'Hasn't *Rob* ever heard of pupil–teacher confidentiality?'

'I'm sure he has, but he also knows I have a special interest in you,' Leo said evenly.

Sean glared at him. 'If I want to go and see Zack, then I will – I don't have to listen to *you*!' my brother spat out.

If Leo was hurt by Sean's reaction he didn't show it. But his voice got a lot firmer as he said, 'Sean, when your mum's not here I'm in charge and you *do* have to listen to me. So you can text Zack to say you're not coming, then you can eat your dinner, do your homework, watch some TV and by then I reckon it'll be time for you to go to bed. Though you can always skip the TV and go to bed a bit earlier if you carry on with the attitude.'

Sean narrowed his eyes and even I found myself staring at Leo in disbelief. Was he really threatening to send my brother to bed early if he didn't behave?

'*Unbelievable!*' Sean spat at him. 'And I thought you were cool!' And he stomped off angrily upstairs.

Leo's sternness seemed to evaporate the second my brother left the room. 'Crikey, what's got into *him*?' He seemed more bemused than anything.

'He'll be all right in a bit,' I attempted to reassure him. 'It's just that Mum doesn't usually . . .' I trailed off, not sure quite how to say it, and knowing that it was only half the problem in any case.

'She doesn't lay down the law like that?' Leo suggested. As I nodded, he sighed. 'Maybe I *did* sound a bit like a Victorian parent . . .'

I shrugged. 'It's OK. I wouldn't sweat about it. Though I do see his point about Mr Mann.'

'How do you mean?'

'Well, when we're at school you want us to treat you like any other teacher, right?'

'Of course.'

'But you're not treating Sean like any other pupil if you're discussing him like that with Mr Mann.'

And I went upstairs, leaving him looking thoughtful.

In my bedroom I closed the door behind me and went over to stand in front of the mirror. What Lily had said at Blossom House had really got me thinking. Was it true that I needed to be more image conscious? Was I actually starting to *look* dorky?

Of course my shoes (which I'd left downstairs) were undisputedly high in dork factor, but when I stared critically at the rest of what I was wearing I didn't think I looked too bad. OK, so my school skirt isn't as short as some people's and I suppose I do look a bit shapeless with my shirt so loosely tucked into the waistband of my skirt, but at least it hides the fact that I'm so flat chested. I don't think my *face* looks dorky. I mean, I don't wear glasses with thick lenses or have my hair scraped back off my face or look like some mini professor (the way Jillian does).

But I suppose being a dork isn't just about *looking* odd. It's about how you behave as well. Being a chess champion is definitely dorky. Being uber-swotty at school is pretty dorky. I wasn't so sure about writing poems all the time as a hobby, but I suppose some people might think that's dorky. But what about just being friends with those people? Did that count as dorky too?

I was still thinking about it when Leo called upstairs to tell us that dinner was ready. It smelt yummy. Sean, however, didn't budge from his room.

Not relishing another showdown between the two of them, and with no sign of Mum returning home any time soon, I decided to take charge of the situation. After all, it's not just Lily who's capable of telling people things for their own good that they really don't want to hear.

'Sean, just because you're upset about Monty, you shouldn't take it out on Leo,' I told him as I stood in his doorway. When he still didn't move off his bed, I added, 'Listen, Sean, you were right about one thing . . .' I paused to make sure I had his full attention. 'You were right when you told Leo he's *not* our dad!'

Sean gave me a startled sort of look. 'I didn't say that!'

'No, but he knew that's what you meant when you told him you don't have to listen to him! And anyway, you were right. He's *not* our dad. He doesn't actually owe us anything. So if you're mean to him he can leave any time he likes!'

We both knew what would happen if Leo left. Mum would shut the curtains and go to bed for weeks. It would be like when she found out the truth about Married Michael – home would be dark and cold and miserable. So even though it was hard having Leo telling us what to do, surely it was better than going back to how things were before?

I don't know for sure if it was my little intervention that did the trick, but in any case Sean joined us soon after Leo and I had started to eat.

Sean was flushing a little as he stood awkwardly just inside the kitchen door. 'Sorry,' he muttered.

'Come and eat your dinner before it gets cold,' Leo told him calmly. As my brother sat he added, 'Listen, you can't expect me *not* to care how you're doing at school, OK?'

When Sean didn't say anything I kicked him sharply under the table. If he didn't want to lose Leo, then he was just going to have to suck it up when Leo went all parental on him.

'Yes, Leo,' Sean trotted out in reply, before shooting me a glare as if to say, *Happy now?*

Leo looked curiously at both of us and I could tell he was wondering what he'd missed, but the only thing he said was, 'Good boy,' before launching into a funny story about school.

Chapter Twelve

The following afternoon I was walking out of school with Priti at the end of the day, when who should appear in front of us but Rafferty.

'Hi, Sasha,' he said with a grin.

I think I went bright red from head to toe as soon as he spoke to me. And finally I understood what was going on. I was having my first proper crush on a boy – on my best friend's older brother. Oh my God! I've known Raffy since I was tiny. Once, when I was five, he tickled me so much that I actually wet myself. How could this be happening? And how could I stop him – or Lily – from finding out?

Raffy's tie was pushed casually to one side and his top three shirt buttons were undone. I couldn't help staring guiltily at the Union Jack vest he was sporting underneath his shirt. Then I had a horrible thought.

I know Lily's dad has a very hairy chest because I saw it once at a barbecue. What if that sort of thing runs in families? I wasn't sure I could handle it if Raffy turned out to be that hairy too. Still, there was no hair poking out the top of his vest right now, thank goodness.

'Oh . . . hi, Raffy,' I just about got out without choking. 'Nice chest . . . I mean *vest*!'

'See you tomorrow, Sasha,' Priti said with a little giggle as she left the two of us alone together.

'Your face is really red, Sasha. Are you OK?' Raffy sounded genuinely concerned, as if he honestly thought I might have a bad case of sunburn, or be running some weird fever or something.

I nodded, not trusting myself to speak.

'Lily told me about your snake problem,' he continued.

That struck me as a bit odd, because Lily herself had barely spoken to me all day and had left me to hang out with Priti and Jillian. But if she'd told Raffy about Monty, maybe she still wanted to help me after all.

I tried to sound casual as I murmured, 'Er . . . yes . . .'

'It's a python, right?'

I nodded.

'Cool.'

I just smiled stupidly and nodded again.

'Lily said it got lost in this Blossom House place where you and Sean have been hanging out?'

This time I glanced round quickly to check no one was listening and he seemed to get the hint.

'Hey, I get it. It's a secret, right? I should think what you're doing is pretty *illegal*, huh?'

'Um . . . maybe . . .' I saw that he was taking his chewing gum out to offer me some – taking it out of the packet, I mean, not out of his mouth. 'No, thanks,' I said, then started worrying in case that sounded rude. Fortunately, before I could over-think the whole chewing gum thing, Rafferty spoke again.

'So . . . if you like I'll come to Blossom House with you now and help you look for your snake,' he offered.

'Really?' I just about fainted on the spot.

'Sure.' Rafferty's gaze was directed expectantly at me as he waited for an answer.

'Well . . . OK,' I said awkwardly. 'Thanks.' It was hard trying to sound casual. 'I need to find Sean first though. He already went to have a look for Monty before school so he's got the key with him. He'll probably want to come with us.'

I knew Sean would be in no rush to get home after the way Mum had torn into him when she'd got back from work the evening before. She'd been furious with him for showing her up in front of her clients and she'd shown no signs of forgiving him by breakfast.

But when I found Sean in the playground he just handed over the keys and wished me luck. Zack had been off sick that day, so Sean was going round to his house straight after school to tell him about Monty.

Before I knew what was happening, Raffy and I were walking to Blossom House together. Raffy was listening to music and every time I glanced sideways at him he looked perfectly at ease with the fact that he was totally ignoring me. At first I felt a bit alarmed by our lack of communication, but then I reminded myself that this could easily be the sort of 'comfortable silence' Mum always says is just as important in a relationship as stimulating conversation.

At last we arrived outside Blossom House, where Raffy quickly put his earbuds in his pocket and gave the place his full attention.

'Wow! This is amazing!' he exclaimed as we walked together down the drive. 'And you guys can really let yourselves inside whenever you like?'

I nodded. 'Follow me.'

After we got through the side gate I paused with my back to the house to give him more of a chance to admire the garden. I was hoping he would make some comment about the cherry blossom trees. Don't ask me why that was so important, but I knew that Raffy was going to go down in my estimation if he didn't appreciate how beautiful they were.

Fortunately he didn't disappoint me. 'Wow! This is really something! And there must be loads of fruit to nick later on, isn't there?'

'Well ... no ... you see, cherry blossom trees are ornamental – you don't actually get any fruit.'

'Really? That's a bummer.' He turned his attention to the house. 'What a shame this whole place is just going to waste.'

'I know,' I said. I didn't want to disagree with him. 'But now someone's about to buy it. That's why we have to find Monty as quickly as possible. Before the house isn't ours any more.' Luckily Monty hadn't made an appearance during Mum's viewing the day before, and thankfully the couple weren't interested anyway. But Miranda's client had called her again this week to confirm that he was still very keen and was going to make an offer.

As I led Raffy inside, I asked, 'Shall I show you the room he escaped from?'

'Show me the room you showed Lily yesterday,' he said eagerly.

I noticed that his eyes were everywhere as we moved through the hall and into the main reception room, where he immediately started wowing just like Lily had. He walked over to look in the mirror, then began to walk round the periphery of the room, hunching down to examine the skirting boards. I thought he was looking for potential snake holes until I realised he was inspecting the plug sockets.

'What are you doing that for?' I asked.

He turned to me with a delighted sparkle in his eyes. His eyes were light brown like Lily's but they had little flecks of green in them too. I couldn't believe I'd never noticed the exact colour of his eyes before.

'Lily's right,' he said. 'This *would* be the perfect place to hold our party!'

'What?' Suddenly I realised what he meant. 'No way, Raffy,' I told him firmly. 'I already said no to Lily.'

But he completely ignored me and carried on talking. 'You know we can't have the party at our place any more, don't you, Sasha? But we could easily swop the venue to here. You wouldn't need to arrange anything – we'll do all that. Come on, Sasha! It'll make my day if you let us! Not just my day – my whole year! No, forget that . . . I mean my whole *life*!' He was being so dramatic that he soon had me laughing. 'Come on, Sasha. Do it for *me*! *Please?*' He put one hand on my shoulder and I immediately felt shivery goosebumps prick the back of my neck. As he gazed at me with a genuinely pleading expression in his eyes, I found my resolve starting to melt.

'But is it safe? I mean what about Monty? What if we haven't found him by then?'

'It doesn't matter. It's not like he's dangerous. Anyway he won't come out with all that noise going on. Come on, Sasha . . . Lily said you'd be too scared to help us, but I told her you're way gutsier than she thinks. You've got to prove me right! Come on!'

'I don't know . . .' I murmured. I knew I should say no. In fact I already *had* said no. But I liked that he thought I was gutsy.

'I'll owe you big time,' he said. '*Please*, Sasha?' His big melty eyes seemed to hold mine for an extra-long moment. It was like being faced with the adorable puppy of your dreams and the really hunky boy of your dreams all rolled into one.

'OK, then,' I heard myself say a little shakily.

OK? Did I just say OK?

Apparently I had, because now Raffy was giving me a huge grin and the sparkle in his eyes as he looked into mine made me feel like I was flying. I had to remind myself that he was fifteen and I was only nearly thirteen, and he probably still thought of me as his kid sister's dorky friend.

'I knew you'd say yes!' he exclaimed with a happy laugh. 'I'll tell Lily and we can start to plan everything. You really are the best, Sasha!'

And in a flash he was out through the back door before I even registered that he'd totally forgotten to help me look for Monty. But I still couldn't stop smiling.

Chapter Thirteen

Needless to say, Zack was pretty upset when Sean told him the news about Monty, although he didn't blame Sean. Snakes are great escape artists apparently, and Zack felt it was partly his fault for not warning us properly.

'Zack says snakes are nocturnal, so we might have to sneak into Blossom House after dark one night and wait for Monty to show up – a sort of snake stake-out!' Sean joked on the way to school the next morning.

'Well, so long as you catch him before Saturday,' I said.

'Why Saturday?'

And that's when I broke the news to him about the party. I tried to be really casual, like it was no big deal, like I offered up Blossom House as a party venue for Year Tens all the time.

'WHAT?' Sean just about exploded. He ranted on and on at me about how he couldn't believe I'd said yes to the party without even asking him.

'Hey, *you* took Zack to Blossom House without asking *me*!' I retaliated defensively.

'That was Zack. This is half the school!'

'I'm sure it won't be that many, Sean! Lighten up, will you?'

'*Lighten up?* Come on, Sasha! This doesn't even sound like *you* talking! You don't have to say yes to this just to impress Lily and her mates, you know!'

'I'm not doing it to impress Lily!' I snapped back.

'Then *why?*' he demanded.

Of course I couldn't tell him the truth.

'Because Sensible Sasha has taken a hike!' I declared with a grin, not really caring whether or not he believed me.

In school I seemed to be everybody's favourite person all of a sudden, thanks to Lily spreading the word that I was the one providing the new party venue. Everything seemed to be back to normal between me and Lily, and anyone who hadn't yet been invited to the party was seeking me out to present his or her case. And I had to admit it was swelling my head a bit. I don't think

I'd ever had a reason to feel this important before at school. I mean, I'd always done well academically, and it felt good each time I got praised by a teacher for getting a good grade. But as for feeling *socially* important – never!

Rafferty had been texting people all day to make sure everybody knew about the change in venue. Lily and I were allowed to invite ten friends between us. Everyone was going to tell their parents that the party was being held at the house of 'a girl in another class' and if asked they were to give her name as Blossom. (Needless to say, Blossom's parents would be staying upstairs for the entire time, which was why they wouldn't be meeting and greeting any parents who were dropping off or picking up their kids.)

'We'll have to make sure we remove that FOR SALE sign from out front,' Lily kept reminding me.

'You mean the UNDER OFFER sign,' I said gloomily, because the man Miranda had shown round had just had his offer accepted. Soon the sign would say SOLD. I was trying not to think about how I'd feel when Blossom House was totally off limits for us. In a way I should be looking at this as a sort of a goodbye party, I thought, only I was afraid that if I did I wouldn't enjoy it so much.

One of the good things about agreeing to have the party at Blossom House was that I could invite Priti and Jillian.

Priti agreed at once to come, though Jillian said no because she didn't like big parties. To be honest, I was quite relieved about Jillian because I had a feeling that if she came she might cramp my style pretty badly (even if, according to Lily, I don't have much of it to cramp).

Lily looked surprised when I told her Priti was coming, but she didn't put up any fuss. I had a feeling Lily was in for an even bigger surprise on the night of the party. I'd been to a family birthday party with Priti when one of her cousins turned twenty-one. She'd worn her hair loose instead of the scraped-back way she always wears it at school and she'd looked amazing, boogying away on the dance floor with all her older cousins.

'Sasha, what are you going to wear on Saturday?' Lily asked me. 'Do you want to borrow something of mine?'

'Thanks, Lily, but you know your stuff won't fit me.'

'Some of it will,' Lily persisted. 'You're a bit curvier on top now than you used to be. When my mum saw you the other day she said she could definitely see that you were starting to develop. She thinks you should speak to your mum about getting a bra.'

'Lily!' I felt my face flush bright red. Trust Lily to bring that up in the middle of the school playground.

'Sorry,' she said with a grin. 'Listen, a few of the girls are coming over to mine for a couple of hours tonight. Why don't you come too? We're going to do our nails and stuff. It'll be really cool. And you can try on a couple of my things.'

'*Which* girls?' I asked warily.

'Clara and Hanna and Ellie.'

'Oh . . . well . . . I don't know,' I murmured uncertainly. The fact that the others were going to be there put me off. Though there was one other factor to consider. 'What about Raffy?' I asked her as casually as I could.

'What about him?' She was giving me a funny look and I knew I'd have to be careful if I didn't want her to guess exactly how I felt about her brother.

'Well, shouldn't we be getting together with *him* as well, so we can make plans for the party?'

'Oh yeah . . . well . . . it all seems to be under control. Raffy says he'll take his docking station for the music and we can go to the pound shop to get some drinks and snacks beforehand.'

I took a deep breath. 'I still want to ask him a couple of things. I want to make sure we won't get caught.'

'Well, you can speak to him tonight if you like. Normally I wouldn't recommend it, but he'll probably be quite civil since it's you.'

Since it's you. Just hearing those three words put my head into a sudden crazy spin. But of course she probably didn't mean that Raffy thought of me as special – just that he knew he needed to keep on my good side if he wanted to hold his party at Blossom House.

I ended up being the last of Lily's guests to arrive that evening – probably because I'd changed what I was wearing about six times before setting off. Even though it was just an evening at Lily's place, I still didn't feel comfortable with the others and I hated the thought that they might all be talking about how I looked.

Clara, Hanna and Ellie were all sitting on Lily's bedroom floor gossiping about boys when Lily took me upstairs. As they chatted they were trying out nail polish samples that Ellie had brought with her.

'Sasha, do you think Sean likes Hanna?' Clara asked me with a wicked grin the second I walked in.

I looked at Hanna in surprise, noticing that she was flushing furiously as she told Clara to shut up.

'Well . . .' I answered, trying to adjust to the idea of anyone fancying my brother, who isn't really into girls yet – at least not as far as I know. 'I guess I could ask him for you . . .'

'No way!' Hanna screeched.

'OK, I won't!' I had to admit I'd have died if Lily had ever asked Raffy if he liked *me*. 'I didn't know you even *knew* Sean that well, Hanna!'

'She doesn't. That's probably why she fancies him!' Clara quipped.

I gave Clara a challenging look. 'What's *that* supposed to mean?'

'Nothing! It was a joke. Can't you take a joke?'

I turned away from her feeling my blood boiling. I really didn't like Clara.

'I think he'd be flattered if he knew you liked him,' Lily told Hanna. 'Though he might be too embarrassed to admit it at first. You should try and hang out with him at the party.'

'Oh, Sean's not coming to the party,' I told them, then wished I hadn't as they all started asking why, and Hanna looked pretty gutted. 'Oh . . . it's just that we had a row about it. It's no big deal. He might even change his mind and come in the end.'

'Mum's got drinks and cream cakes for us downstairs. I'll go and fetch them,' Lily said, moving towards the door.

I quickly volunteered to go with her.

As the two of us went downstairs, I asked her, 'Why does Clara always have to be so bitchy?'

'She's not *always* bitchy,' Lily replied matter-of-factly. 'It's mostly just when you're around.'

'Oh, well, that's great,' I murmured.

'She won't admit it but I think she's jealous because she knows you're still my best friend.'

'Really?' It hadn't occurred to me that Lily would have told Clara that I *was* still her best friend. I must say, I'd sort of fudged the issue with Priti and told her that she and Lily were *both* my besties.

In the kitchen we found Rafferty eating a chocolate éclair.

'Hey!' Lily exclaimed angrily. 'Mum got those in for *us*!' She went to the fridge and flung open the door to find a box of four pastries instead of five. 'You greedy pig! You already had a donut!'

'I know, but I was still hungry and I thought at least one of you was bound to be on a diet,' he teased.

'Lily, it's OK. We can cut them all up and share out the pieces,' I suggested hastily.

'See,' Rafferty said. 'Sasha isn't making a drama out of it – *she's* staying cool and coming up with an intelligent solution. You could learn a lot from – ouch!' He yelped as Lily hit him on the arm.

'It's no wonder you're getting such a big fat bum,' Lily hissed at him.

'I am not.'

'Yes, you are. Isn't he, Sasha?'

Being asked to give my opinion on Rafferty's bum completely threw me off guard. I felt the colour rush to my cheeks as I gazed in a sort of daze at the jean-clad object under discussion. Why was this happening to me? Surely Lily would notice.

'Oh, I . . . I don't know . . .' I stammered as I left Lily to sort out the pastries and rushed back upstairs.

'Sasha, didn't you want to ask Raffy something about the party?' Lily called after me.

'Later!' I yelled back, diving into the bathroom in a desperate attempt to grab some time alone to compose myself.

'Sasha, do you want any help with your make-up?' Ellie asked me half an hour later when we'd all finished doing our nails.

Clara and Hanna had already had their eyes done. Actually they both looked pretty good, though Clara had added loads of black eyeliner to hers afterwards, which made her look like a bit of a Goth.

'You know, you've got lovely clear skin, Sasha,' Ellie told me.

'My mum says it's normal for your skin to get bad when you have your period,' Clara said as she carefully applied some concealer to the big spot on her chin. 'Sasha hasn't even *started* her periods yet, have you, Sasha?'

I found myself flushing from ear to ear. Oh my God, had all of them started already then? Had every girl in my year at school started except me? Was I some kind of freak now?

'It's probably because Sasha was a premature baby,' Lily said, rushing to my defence and making things ten times worse as usual. 'I mean, it's not her fault if she's a bit behind in her development.'

Ellie saw me cringing and said, 'I don't think she *is* behind though, Lily. Lots of girls our age haven't started their periods yet.'

'My cousin in Poland didn't start *hers* until she was sixteen,' Hanna volunteered.

'Yeah, but that doesn't count,' Clara said dismissively. 'Everybody probably starts their periods later in Poland.'

'Huh?' Hanna looked bemused.

'That's a pretty racist thing to say, Clara,' I said solemnly.

'What?' Clara looked taken aback.

'Well, it's kind of implying that Poland is a backwards country,' I pointed out, trying not to look too smug as I took my revenge.

'*Is* that what you're saying, Clara?' Hanna demanded crossly.

Clara was the one to blush then. 'Of course not . . . I just meant . . . well, it's not such a *rich* country, is it? And there aren't as many jobs . . . and well . . . it's freezing cold there in the winter and you guys eat different food . . . and who knows how all that affects your hormones and stuff . . .' She trailed off, and I'm ashamed to say I felt pretty gleeful watching her squirm.

'You know, you really ought to count to ten before you open your mouth sometimes, Clara,' Lily said with a frown.

'Yes,' Hanna snapped. 'You totally *should*!'

'Sorry,' Clara mumbled before rapidly trying to make amends by offering to help Hanna reshape her eyebrows. 'Not that they need reshaping!' she added quickly when Hanna looked even crosser.

'You're right. They don't,' Hanna agreed. 'But *yours* do. Sasha, pass me those tweezers, will you?'

I know it's wrong to enjoy other people's pain, but it was a superhuman effort not to laugh at the look on Clara's face. And I had to admit that this whole hanging-out-with-the-girls thing was turning out to be a lot more fun than I'd thought.

'Ellie, you are *so* lucky having a mum who's a beautician,' Lily gushed a bit later as she rummaged through the lipsticks Ellie had brought with her to find the boldest colour. 'Hey, have you got a good mascara for Sasha? God knows she could use one.'

'Gee thanks, Lily,' I said, pulling a face as Ellie laughed.

'Go and look at yourself in the bathroom mirror, Sasha. The light's better in there,' Ellie said when she'd finished making me up with mascara and eyeliner and two different eye shadows.

So I went to the bathroom and switched on the light.

'Wow!' I whispered as I stared at the new me. I looked older and more sophisticated somehow.

I could have stood staring at myself in that mirror for ages, and I briefly wondered what Mum would think if she could see me.

More to the point, what would *Raffy* think?

Before I could change my mind, I left the bathroom and went to knock on Rafferty's bedroom door, remembering how when Lily and I were younger we used to sneak into his room uninvited all the time and giggle hysterically as he yelled at us to get out.

I swallowed hard and tried to stay calm as one sentence kept repeating itself over and over inside my head. *You have to act normally. You have to act normally. You have to act normally.*

The door opened and Raffy stood there, looking extremely surprised to see me.

'Sasha?' He was peering at me with a bit of a frown but he didn't comment on my makeover.

'Um . . . it's about the party . . .' I practically choked out.

'Oh . . . right . . .' He beckoned me further into his room but didn't shut the door. I couldn't help looking around. It was even messier than Sean's bedroom, and that was saying something.

My eyes locked on to his school clothes, discarded in an untidy heap on the floor by his bed – grey jumper, white shirt, school tie, grey trousers, sweaty-looking socks . . . thankfully no underpants.

'So what is it?' he grunted, self-consciously kicking his dirty clothes further under the bed.

'Oh, um . . . it's just, I was wondering . . . How are we going to make sure Blossom House doesn't get trashed on Saturday?' I asked in a rush.

'Oh, don't worry about that,' he said. 'You know we've only invited half the people we were going to ask before, right?'

'So . . . you've invited *fifty*?'

He nodded. 'Give or take.'

'I still think fifty is quite a lot,' I said nervously.

'They probably won't all come, Sasha. And they definitely won't all come at the same time. In fact I reckon there'll be people coming and going all night!'

I frowned. Somehow that didn't make me feel any better.

'But what if . . . well . . .' I trailed off nervously.

'Is this about the W.C.S.?'

'Huh?'

He sighed. 'Sorry. That's Lily-speak for Worst Case Scenario. Lily said you'd want to know about it.'

'Oh . . . well, it's just . . . what if anyone, well . . .'

'Throws up?' he supplied for me. 'Nicks something? Breaks a window? Shakes up all the fizzy drinks bottles and sprays them all over the room?'

'You really think all *that* could happen?' I asked, suddenly feeling a bit ill.

He reached out and calmly patted me on the shoulder. 'It *could* happen, Sasha, but I won't let it. Trust me. You're gonna have a great time. You just leave everything to me.'

He gave me his biggest, warmest smile, and in those few seconds all my worries melted away.

Chapter Fourteen

I got back from Lily's house just after half past nine (Ellie and I walked back together) to find Leo standing drinking coffee in the kitchen with Mum, who'd just got back from her yoga class.

'Sasha!' Mum exclaimed. 'What happened to my little girl?' That was a first. Like I said before, Mum's not usually one to worry about how quickly I'm growing up.

I'd forgotten for a moment that I hadn't taken off my make-up. Plus my hair was all gelled up and had silver glitter sprinkled in it and I was wearing a mini skirt Lily had given me because it was too small for her.

'Yikes! You look like a deranged pop star,' Sean said, coming into the kitchen behind me and handing Leo a book. 'This is it, Leo. I mean, basically it was really dull and I hated it! Can't I just write *that* for the book report? I only chose it because it was the shortest book there.

Talking about *short* . . .' Sean was staring pointedly at my skirt.

'Get lost,' I said defensively.

'That skirt is one of Lily's, isn't it?' Mum said. 'I seem to remember that when Lily wore it she also wore tights.'

'It's too warm for tights, Mum! Anyway, Lily says the whole point is to show off my legs.'

'Sasha, you're twelve!'

'Nearly thirteen,' I said huffily.

'Let's leave the ladies alone to discuss this, shall we?' Leo said, whisking my brother off into the living room.

As soon as they were gone, Mum said, 'Well, you'd better not let Granny see it. She'll probably start looking for a hem to let down.'

'Is Granny still coming?' I asked. I'd almost forgotten, so much had been going on since we got back to school. My stomach lurched a bit at the thought of Granny arriving in the middle of our party plans. She's always the first to sniff out any hint of trouble.

She nodded. 'Tomorrow. I can't say I'm looking forward to introducing her to Leo.'

'Don't worry about it,' I said. 'We've told Leo what she's like. He's not going to blame you, no matter how rude she is to him.'

Mum sighed. 'Did I ever tell you about the day I first introduced her to your dad?'

'No,' I said, my ears instantly pricking up. I love it when she talks about our dad. 'What happened?'

'We were both only twenty-one. We'd been putting off the whole meet-the-parents thing while we were still students, but then we decided to go travelling together and we knew we couldn't postpone it any longer.' She paused. 'He was the first boyfriend I'd been really serious about and your granny gave him the Spanish Inquisition of course. She asked him how he planned to pay the bills and look after me – and we weren't even engaged or anything! I was terrified he'd run away and never come back. My father did his best to help us, bless him. He took your dad up to the spare room and showed him his magician's trunk. Not that that pleased your granny when she found out!'

'Granny still hates the fact that Grandpa was a magician, doesn't she?' I said. 'Last time she was here Sean asked her whether she ever acted as his assistant and let Grandpa cut her in half. You should've seen her face!'

Mum said with a little laugh, 'I wish I had.'

'But why is she so ashamed of it, Mum? Being a magician is cool!'

'That's what I always thought.' Mum gave a rueful smile.

'She doesn't even have any photos of him up in her house.'

Mum sighed. 'I know. It's as if she's ashamed of him as a person, not just the magician part. I don't understand it either. The trouble is Granny can be such a snob about certain things.' She sighed. 'Poor Leo has no idea what he's letting himself in for. I just hope she doesn't scare him off.'

I didn't say anything, but I thought back to how Granny had rescued us time and again, especially after Dad died and after Married Michael. And I thought about what would happen if Leo ever changed his mind about us.

Granny wasn't so bad, not really. And anyway, the fact was, like it or not, our lives would be way scarier if she wasn't around.

After school the next day, Sean and I had to go and meet Granny at the train station.

As usual our grandmother was the first passenger to disembark and she was instantly recognisable in her bright purple coat and green hat. Granny likes to stand out from the crowd and she always wears colourful scarves, big floppy hats and huge sparkly brooches. (Mum once accused her of standing out a bit too much and Granny snapped back, 'Well, why ever not? After all, you're a long time dead!' Which is true, I guess, though only Granny would actually come out and say it.)

'Granny!' Sean called the second we spotted her.

My brother always seems to regress by several years whenever our grandmother comes to stay, and this time was no exception. As soon as Granny stepped out through the ticket barrier he immediately started jumping around her like a five-year-old, trying to sneak a look inside her large canvas shopping bag for the Easter eggs he knew she'd have brought with her since we hadn't seen her at all over the holiday. Granny immediately smacked his hand away and ordered him to stop being so silly and to give her a proper hug.

Mum wasn't due home from work for another hour and we had orders to take Granny back to the house and to make sure we carried her bags. So we set off, with me dragging her little wheelie suitcase and Sean carrying her shopping bag.

'So,' Granny said as she took out a crumpled paper bag of Murray mints and popped one in her mouth before offering them to us. 'How is your mother? Has she seen

sense yet and broken off her engagement to that . . .
that . . . ridiculously young man?'

'Leo isn't *ridiculously* young, Granny,' I said. 'And he's
really nice. I bet you'll like him when you get to know
him.'

'Yeah, Granny. Leo's cool,' Sean backed me up.

'Cool?' Granny repeated crisply. 'Well, yes . . . that's
what I was afraid of.'

It was just as well Leo had decided *not* to spend that
evening with us, I thought with a sigh. Though on the
other hand, there was something to be said for getting
stressful things over and done with. As it was, the big
event wouldn't happen until Saturday, when we were all
going out for lunch together to 'break the ice', as Mum
had put it.

Just then my phone rang. It was Mum asking if we'd
collected Granny yet. Then she explained that Miranda
wanted Blossom House completely cleared of all remain-
ing personal items and rubbish. Miranda was doing it as a
favour to the owner, and since Mum owed *her* a few
favours she had agreed to help. They were going there
straight after work to get started.

When I related what she'd said to the others, Granny
frowned and I thought she was going to complain that

Mum wasn't giving her much of a welcome. Instead she said, 'Did you just say this place was named *Blossom House*?'

'That's right.'

'And where is it?'

'It's in the street just behind ours – the one with all the trees and the big Victorian houses.'

Granny narrowed her eyes. 'Which street exactly?'

I told her the street name and Granny scowled even more.

'Do you know it then?' Sean asked curiously. Granny had never mentioned knowing anyone who lived there. Of course she had old friends from before she moved away, but they were mostly on the other side of town where her house used to be.

'What? No, of course not!' Granny replied fiercely.

Like I've said before, I've always been good at guessing what other people are thinking, and I'm also pretty good at picking up when they're lying to me. And I was definitely getting the feeling that Granny was hiding something.

'I know,' I said. 'Let's go round to Blossom House to help Mum and Miranda. Granny, you can come too, if you want.'

'Why on earth would I want to do that?' Granny replied sharply. 'I shall go home and start preparing our dinner since your mother clearly hasn't given it any thought. You two go if you want to, and tell your mother not to be too late back unless she wants a totally ruined supper.'

I looked at Sean, who quickly nodded. It was definitely in our interests to be at Blossom House when the place was being cleared. We could have another look for Monty and hopefully spot him before anyone else did if he came out of hiding. We could also remove anything that we didn't want to be found – like Monty's box and heat mat for instance.

'We'll walk you home first, Granny,' I said quickly. And I found myself wondering what my chances were of being allowed to take home those beautiful 1950s dresses if I pretended to discover them while we were helping to clear the place out.

Chapter Fifteen

Much to my surprise it was Leo who greeted us when we arrived at Blossom House. He quickly explained that Mum had recruited him to help out too, and that Mum and Miranda had been delayed at work.

After enquiring (rather nervously) about Granny, Leo assigned us the task of emptying out the rickety old shed at the bottom of the garden. The shed had always been locked before, but that week Miranda had finally found the key to the padlock.

'I just need to go and use the loo first,' Sean said, and while I kept Leo talking he went upstairs where I knew he was going to look for Monty. We were both worried in case Monty showed himself to one of the adults while the house was being cleared.

Sean joined me in the back garden after Leo had gone to sort out the garage. He was holding Monty's box and heat pad. 'No sign of him,' he muttered glumly.

'What about the dresses?'

'They're still there. You'd better grab them now if you want them.'

'I'll have to check with Miranda first,' I said. 'Come on. Let's go and get started on the shed.'

Inside the shed we found a lot of discarded junk, including an old birdcage and a large box covered with an old sheet. When Sean pulled off the sheet an old dark-blue metal trunk was revealed.

'That looks a bit like the one in Mum's photograph,' I said. 'You know – the magician's trunk.'

Sean nodded but he was clearly more concerned with what was inside the box, which was locked with a chunky padlock.

'I'm going to fetch those old tools from under the stairs and see if I can get it open,' he told me.

While he was gone I squatted down beside the box to examine the sides more closely. That's when I spotted the gold stars. They were very faded and it was difficult to make them out in the dim light inside the shed, but they were definitely there.

This box was *exactly* like the one our grandfather had owned!

Sean soon came back with the tools, including a metal saw that he thought might cut through the padlock. (I should probably mention that Married Michael was a DIY buff and he'd spent loads of time with my brother, showing him how to do stuff around the house using his impressive collection of tools.)

'Right, then. Here goes.' Sean set to work with confidence but after less than a minute the saw flew out of his hands and landed on the floor. 'Stupid thing!' he hissed.

'Do you want some help? Leo might be able to do it,' I suggested. Not that Leo's DIY skills are anything to celebrate. Once he'd tried to put up a new curtain rail in my bedroom and I'd had to scream for Mum to come and stop him as he started his sixth attempt at drilling a hole in my wall.

'No, I can do it.' Sean picked up the saw and started again, really leaning on the thing now. This time when the blade slipped, it nicked his other hand, making him yelp.

'Let me see.' I grabbed his hand to examine the cut, dragging him back outside where the light was better.

Since Sean is used to me fussing over him whenever he hurts himself he gave in to my examination without too much protest.

He didn't speak until I pulled out a tissue from my pocket to dab at the wound, which didn't appear to be too deep, thank goodness.

'I hope that's a clean tissue,' he grunted sourly.

'Nah, it's covered in snot!'

Just then we heard Leo calling and we looked up to see him coming towards us through the trees.

Straight away Leo homed in on the bloodied tissue Sean was holding. 'What happened?'

'It's OK. Sasha already checked it and . . . hey!'

Leo had taken hold of his wrist and now he was inspecting the wound, which was still oozing blood at a steady rate. 'How did you do it?' he asked when he'd satisfied himself that the cut wasn't deep enough for stitches. As he spoke he replaced the tissue and began pressing down on it himself.

'It was an accident,' Sean mumbled. 'The saw slipped.'

'*Saw?*'

Seeing his frown, Sean immediately went on the defensive. 'Michael always let me use his tools!'

'Michael?' Leo looked confused (possibly because Mum only ever refers to Michael as 'that two-timing rat' or 'that utter snake-in-the-grass').

'*Married* Michael,' I explained quickly, hoping that would jog his memory.

'Oh . . . right.' Leo gave my brother a serious look. 'Listen, Sean, I don't really care what Michael did or didn't let you do . . . In future I don't want you doing stuff like this without asking me or your mother first.'

'Right . . . like *you'd* be any help,' Sean muttered snippily.

'Oh, I don't know . . . I might be useful for driving you and your finger to A&E if you accidentally cut it off,' Leo retorted. 'What were you trying to saw through in any case?'

We took him inside the shed to show him.

'Those hinges look almost completely rusted through,' I told Sean. 'It might be easier to break *them* off, don't you think?'

'Any more wielding of tools can wait,' Leo said firmly as he pushed my brother out of the shed towards the house. 'Come on. Let's get your hand sorted.'

As we stood in the kitchen (where Sean was obediently holding his injured hand under the cold running

130

water), I asked, 'So how long do you think it'll take to finish clearing everything out?'

'Well, if we spend the whole evening here again tomorrow, I'm hoping that should do it,' Leo said. 'The big pieces of furniture are going to stay in any case.'

'I can't wait to show Mum that trunk,' Sean said as he turned off the tap with his good hand.

'Here. Use this.' Leo handed him a wad of dry kitchen towel to stop him dripping watery blood all over the draining board.

As Leo applied a large plaster to Sean's injured hand, my brother gave him a smug look. 'Leo . . .'

'What?'

'You do realise, don't you, that Mum's going to be desperate to open that trunk as soon as she gets here?'

Sean was right about Mum being just as keen as we were to open the trunk. In fact she was practically bouncing off the walls in her excitement once she saw it. She knew straight away that it was a magician's trunk.

'It's really funny,' she said. 'It's just like my dad's – your grandpa's. He stored all his props in it and used it in his act. I haven't seen one like it since he died.'

We had just been debating the best way to get inside it when Miranda, who had arrived with Mum, miraculously produced the key (apparently it had been on an old set of house keys she kept at the office).

But to everyone's immense disappointment there had turned out to be nothing inside the box. Sean had insisted on checking for a false bottom or a secret compartment, but even after a very careful search he'd still come up with nothing at all.

That said I was way too excited by my three new dresses – which Miranda had agreed I could keep – to feel too disappointed by the empty trunk. When we got home I sent Lily and Ellie photos of each dress and Ellie texted me straight back suggesting that I wore one of them to the party.

I thought it was a brilliant idea, although I was having a difficult time deciding which of the three to choose. My favourite was the red halter neck, but the skirt was too long on me. It might have been OK if I was wearing high heels but I didn't have any, and even if I had I wouldn't have wanted to totter about in them all evening. The emerald dress fitted me well and I liked the way the skirt swished when I spun round. But the boned bodice dug in a bit and I thought the bow on the front was a bit too fussy.

I eventually settled for the third dress. It was less swishy (because of the bead-studded netting over the skirt), but the velvet bodice was more comfortable and very flattering. I don't tend to wear black very much, but now I could see that it suited me and it also made me look older, plus the fuchsia-coloured skirt was really eye-catching.

'You've gotta be kidding!' Sean exclaimed with a smirk when I went downstairs to show Mum and Granny.

I ignored him and gave Mum a little twirl. 'How do I look?'

'Lovely,' she replied with a smile. 'And very grown up.'

'Where's Granny?' I asked.

'She went outside. Actually I'm a bit worried about her.'

'Why?'

'Sean was showing her the sales brochure for Blossom House and pointing out all the pictures he took,' Mum explained. 'She started peering at them with a really funny look on her face. Then she just rushed out.'

'Sean, what did you say to her?' I demanded.

'I didn't say anything!' Sean protested.

'Are you sure?' Mum was frowning at him.

'I'll go and check she's all right, shall I?' I suggested, slipping a cardigan on over my dress and heading for the front door.

I caught up with Granny a short way along our street. It was dark outside and she had stopped on the pavement a few houses along, where she seemed to be staring up at the stars.

'Are you OK, Granny?' I asked her as I caught up.

'What? Oh, it's you, Sasha . . . Yes, I'm fine. Just felt a little peaky all of a sudden.' She shivered and I saw that she'd come out without her coat.

I wasn't really cold so I took off my cardigan and gave it to her.

'Granny, did Sean say something that upset you?' I asked gently.

'Oh no, dear. It wasn't anything Sean said,' she assured me as she began to walk with me back to the house with the cardigan round her shoulders. As we passed under a lamppost she turned to look at me and suddenly froze. 'What are you wearing?'

'It's an old evening dress that came from Blossom House. Miranda said I could have it. Do you like it?'

'*Like* it? Sasha, I want you to go and take off that dreadful old thing and . . . and . . . I never want to see it on you again, do you understand?'

'But, Granny –'

'NEVER!' She yelled it so loudly that the entire street probably heard.

Mum certainly did from where she'd been standing at the front door waiting for us.

'Sasha, what happened?' she asked as I rushed past her into the house.

I was almost in tears. 'She was really horrible to me about this dress.'

'The *dress*? Why?'

'I don't know.'

Mum frowned and I could tell that Granny's behaviour made absolutely no sense to her either.

Chapter Sixteen

There were only thirty-six hours to go until the party and we still hadn't found Monty. Plus I was seriously worried about my grandmother.

'Maybe she's going demented,' Lily suggested help-fully at school when I told her what had happened. 'My great-aunt's demented and she's always shouting at us for no reason and accusing us of stealing her clothes and things.'

'I don't think it's that,' I said. 'Granny's memory seems fine. It was only that *one* thing she said about my dress that didn't make any sense. Mum tried to get her to say what the problem was but she wouldn't. Though she did tell me later that she was sorry for yelling at me.'

'Strange . . . so are you still going to wear that dress to the party?'

'Yep. And Priti's going to wear the red one if it fits her. I'm taking it round to hers after school today so she can try it on.' I had already offered Lily one of the dresses to wear but she had declined, saying that vintage clothes weren't really her thing.

'Priti won't turn up,' Lily said. 'She'll make some excuse at the last minute. You'll see.'

'No, Lily, I think she'll come,' I said. 'She's already got it all planned out.'

Priti had relayed her plan to me the day before: 'I'll tell Dad I'm going to yours for the evening on Saturday and I'll arrange for him to drop me off there. Mum won't be in because she's going to see my auntie, and Dad won't notice I'm all dressed up if I wear my long coat over the top. I'll walk round to Blossom House, stay at the party for a couple of hours, then walk back to your house and be waiting outside when Dad comes to collect me.'

I was actually surprised by how gutsy she was being. Priti never usually broke the rules or disobeyed her parents. I knew this was a really big deal for her.

As for my own cover story, Mum thought I was sleeping over at Lily's place and Lily's mum thought she was staying at mine. Hopefully our mothers wouldn't mention it to each other at any point, though since they hardly see each other these days, I thought it was unlikely.

'I am *so* excited about tomorrow night, Sasha!' Lily exclaimed, slipping one arm through mine. 'You do realise this is going to be the most fun we've had in, like . . . forever!' And she let out a delighted giggle as she teased, 'You know, I'm starting to think I might not lose you to the dorky side after all!'

I had a great time at Priti's house on Friday evening. We'd stopped at mine on the way back from school to pick up the dress, and when Priti tried it on it fitted her perfectly. It turned out she even had a pair of high-heeled red shoes to go with it.

As usual Priti's dad insisted on giving me a lift home at the end of the evening. He actually drove us past Blossom House, and I saw to my surprise that the lights were on. Weird!

I got home to find Sean sitting in the kitchen eating a large slice of Granny's homemade chocolate cake. (One really good thing about Granny coming to stay is that she always does loads of baking.)

'Sean, I just passed Blossom House and I saw –'

'Mum and Granny are round there,' Sean said without looking up from his cake.

'*Granny?*'

'Yeah. She decided she wanted to go and see the place after all. They've been gone ages.'

'Did Mum and Miranda finish clearing it out?'

'Yeah – just as well, because I'm taking Zack round there tomorrow to look for Monty. He's bringing a mouse to try and entice him out. He says snakes are naturally shy, so he's not surprised Monty hasn't shown up while there've been people in the house.'

'Right . . .' I murmured. I couldn't believe I'd almost forgotten about the Monty crisis in all the excitement about the party.

'Don't worry. Zack and I will be well away from the place by the time *you* lot get there,' he added.

'But I thought Zack wanted to look for Monty after dark.'

'Yeah – well, he's hoping it won't come to that.'

'You know, you and Zack could always just come to the party. You could have a look round for Monty at the same time.'

'No, thanks. I don't intend to be anywhere near the place when you get caught and Mum and Leo go ballistic!

139

Though it's going to be quite cool seeing the looks on their faces when they find out *you're* the one responsible and not me!'

Before I could even respond we heard the front door open.

'Granny!' I went through to the hall, where she was taking off her coat. 'What did you think of Blossom House? Did Mum show you the box?'

'What?' She looked a bit dazed.

'Blossom House? You just went to see it, didn't you?'

'Oh, yes, it was . . . it was . . .' She seemed to forget my question before she'd even answered it. 'Actually I'm rather tired. I think I'll go straight to bed.'

I looked quizzically at Sean as Granny moved slowly up the stairs, looking as if all the energy had been drained out of her.

'What is it with Granny and Blossom House?' I murmured.

Sean just shrugged, clearly a lot less intrigued by the situation than I was. And if I'd expected Mum to throw some light on the matter when *she* came home twenty minutes later, I was wrong. It turned out Mum was totally anxious for a different reason. I'd completely forgotten that tomorrow was the Big Lunch. At long last Granny and Leo were going to meet – and Mum was already panicking about it.

That night it took me ages to get to sleep, and on Saturday morning I woke up filled with anxiety and excitement. Lily started sending me texts before I'd even got out of bed, but I knew I wouldn't be able to concentrate fully on preparing for the party until I'd made it through lunch with Leo and Granny.

I also had to hope that Sean and Zack found that snake in time – not that Lily thought a snake on the loose was a good enough reason to cancel our party. It was just that I'd rather not have to worry about Monty making an appearance in addition to everything else.

Mum was worked up too, though of course she didn't know anything about what I was planning for this evening. All *she* was thinking about was lunch.

'Maybe I should have booked something a bit more formal,' she said with a worried frown when Granny was upstairs getting dressed. 'But I know Granny likes the pasta there and –'

'The pizza place is fine, Mum,' I reassured her swiftly.

'Yeah, Mum, pizza's a great idea,' Sean agreed, adding

141

with a grin, 'If it was a steakhouse there'd be way too many sharp knives!'

Mum glared at him. 'Carry on like that and you can stay at home. This is very stressful, Sean. There's nothing to joke about.'

'Come on, Mum. You need to chill out,' Sean said impatiently. 'Do some deep breathing or something.'

'Yes, Mum. It might help,' I agreed.

'Just watch where you do it,' Sean warned. 'You don't want Granny tripping over you and nearly breaking her ankle like she did that time when you were meditating on the kitchen floor.'

'Poor Mum,' I murmured after she'd gone upstairs to meditate in her bedroom. 'She's really worrying about this.'

'Yeah,' Sean agreed. 'She needs to loosen up. I mean, at the end of the day, Granny will still be on her side whether she stays with Leo or not. Granny just wants to make sure Mum's not about to do something stupid, that's all.'

'Yeah, Granny's just trying to protect the three of us as usual,' I agreed.

We were both thoughtful for a few seconds before turning to face each other. 'Poor Leo,' we both said at once.

Granny was unusually quiet when she eventually came downstairs, but I quickly dismissed the idea that she could be worrying about meeting Leo. Though she might have been mentally compiling her list of interrogation questions for him.

Sean had already left the house to meet Zack for their last-ditch mission to rescue Monty, and Mum had just finished her meditation session, which seemed to have calmed her down.

Trying to draw my grandmother out a bit, I asked her, 'Granny, did Mum show you that old trunk we found in the shed at Blossom House the other day?'

There was a momentary pause before Granny replied stiffly, 'I believe she mentioned it, but I had no desire to go traipsing through all that long grass and weeds to look at some old box.'

'I asked Miranda what she knows about it,' Mum told me, as she passed Granny the butter for her toast. 'It turns out it belonged to the old lady's husband. And guess what? He was a magician too!' She turned to Granny. 'No wonder that box reminds me of Dad's! Miranda says the old lady was his assistant as well as his wife. Apparently she was really tiny and a bit of a contortionist, so she was very good at fitting inside small spaces –'

Suddenly Granny clanked her knife down on her plate and demanded, 'Annabel, are you *deliberately* trying to upset me?'

'What?' Mum looked surprised. 'What on earth do you mean?'

Granny narrowed her eyes and announced that she intended to get the first train home after lunch.

'What? But Leo's planning to take us out this afternoon!' Mum protested. Leo had arranged a trip to a nearby stately home where the cakes are to die for.

'I shall meet the boy at lunchtime and that will be quite enough time spent together for both of us, I should think,' Granny replied briskly.

Now it was Mum whose eyes became slats. 'Leo's not a "boy", Mother!'

'Oh, for goodness' sake, Annabel, don't be so touchy! I'd love to hear what the two of you call *me* behind my back. *Your* trouble is you take everything far too personally!'

'Oh yes?' Mum retorted angrily. 'Well, what about you? *You* seemed to take it pretty personally when I was talking about some other magician having a wife who actually *supported* him! You were always so mean about Dad's job!'

At that point you could have heard a pin dropping on our kitchen floor.

I gaped at Mum.

'Yes, well . . . I think I'll just go upstairs and pack now,' Granny said a little shakily.

As Granny left the kitchen I turned to Mum and gave her a stern look.

'Well, it's *true*!' Mum said defensively. 'Your grandpa loved his job. And he was good at it too. He really made me believe in magic.' Mum stopped and I saw that her eyes had filled with tears. 'You know . . . I was away travelling with your dad when your grandpa died. I couldn't even get back for the funeral. And then when I got home, all his stuff was gone. She didn't even wait to see if I wanted anything . . .'

'Maybe she couldn't stand seeing all his things around her when he wasn't ever coming back,' I said, trying to console her with the first thing I could think of. Though I had to admit what Granny had done did sound a bit mean. I'd never really thought before about how Mum still missed her dad, whereas Granny seemed to want to forget that he'd ever existed.

Frankly, I was beginning to think I didn't understand my family at all.

Chapter Seventeen

At a quarter past one Sean and I were waiting inside the pizza place with Leo. My brother and Zack had spent the morning searching Blossom House for Monty to no avail. Now our minds were on the next challenge of the day.

Or 'Granny versus Leo', as Sean had dubbed it.

'I'm starving,' Sean muttered as he stood up to go and inspect the salad bar.

I went with him.

'Might have known Granny would keep him waiting,' Sean said as he prodded the potato salad with the serving spoon.

'He's dressed like it's a school day,' I pointed out as I glanced back at our table, where Leo was sitting rigidly with his eyes glued to the door.

'I know. He could do with losing the tie,' Sean agreed. 'He looks like he's here for a job interview.'

'Poor thing, he's really nervous,' I murmured.

'Yeah,' Sean agreed and there was something in his voice that almost sounded disappointed. 'You'd think he'd be a bit . . . well, braver . . . wouldn't you? I mean, he stood up to Mr Jamieson that time when he bawled him out for wearing trainers to school after he broke his toe. You'd think he could handle Granny!'

'Oh well . . . she's not here yet,' I said, trying to sound more confident than I felt. That's when I saw what my brother was doing. 'Sean, don't,' I warned him, but as usual he ignored me.

You see, whenever we go anywhere with one of those fill-up-your-own-plate buffet systems, Sean sees it as a personal challenge to cram as much food as possible on to his plate. The challenge also includes making it back to our table without spilling anything. He'd failed on that point the last time and the lady at the next table to ours had ended up with her handbag covered in coleslaw. His behaviour really embarrassed Mum (and me) but no matter how cross Mum gets each time, she can't seem to make him stop doing it.

Today Sean had piled up an absolute mountain of food on to his plate and I closed my eyes and sent up a prayer as he set off across the room with the precariously arranged salad stuff looking fit to topple off at any moment.

'Ta-dah!' he announced proudly as he placed the loaded plate down on our table without mishap. It was heaped with pasta salad, rice salad, bean salad, potato salad, coleslaw and just about everything else at the salad bar except for any actual green stuff. He saw Leo's shocked expression and laughed.

'You know what that looks like?' I told my brother in disgust. 'Like the slops container after school dinners.'

Sean just kept laughing.

Just then our waiter arrived with the garlic bread Leo had ordered for us to munch on while we were waiting. Sean was about to dig in – he loves garlic bread – when Leo's hand shot out to grab my brother's wrist.

'You can have some after you've eaten all of that,' he told him, pointing at the grotesque mountain of salad which we all knew my brother had no intention of actually finishing.

I think Sean thought Leo was joking at first.

'Come on, Leo! There's no need to start acting like Granny! She's not going to like you any better for it!' he teased.

Leo remained sombre, raising a finger at him like he was telling off a young child. 'You don't deliberately waste food.'

Sean immediately went on the defensive. 'Especially not if *you're* the one buying it, I suppose? Well, Mum said *she* was going to pay for lunch, so you don't have to worry!'

'Sean, shut up,' I hissed at him.

Leo was looking angrily at my brother. 'Sean, do you ever watch the news? Because I can't believe you're completely unaware of what goes on in other parts of the world . . . the *developing* world, for example . . .'

My brother instantly looked uncomfortable. I mean it was easy to see where Leo was going with this.

'*You don't deliberately waste food,*' Leo repeated just as sternly as when he'd said it the first time. He paused for a moment, giving Sean a searching look. 'Do you?'

Sean didn't answer him.

'Do you?' Leo repeated, glaring at my brother.

Sean looked like he was finding it hard to swallow.

And right at that moment Granny and Mum arrived.

Leo jumped up straight away and started shaking Granny's hand as Mum did the introductions and apologised for being late.

Granny sat down next to me and immediately started to stare at Leo like she was examining an item in a shop, trying to decide whether or not it was worth buying. I could see Leo beginning to go a bit pink under her scrutiny.

I winced as Sean dug his fork a bit too vigorously into the food mountain on his plate and accidentally dislodged the entire potato salad section, which tumbled half on to the table and half into my brother's lap. I saw him glance warily at Leo, and I saw Granny noticing the glance.

Mum suddenly shoved back her chair saying she needed to use the ladies' room. That was typical of Mum – opting out as soon as the going got tough. I felt a bit cross with her as I watched her leave the table. After all, this had to be way more difficult for Leo than it was for her. I mean, *she* wasn't the one being inspected by Granny.

Suddenly Sean whispered to Leo, 'I'm sorry.'

Leo nodded. 'Eat half of it,' he said quietly.

'OK.' Sean was looking relieved.

That's when I noticed the expression on Granny's face changing slightly. There was a flicker of surprise as she looked at Sean, then Leo, then back again, as if she was reassessing something or other. Then she reached out and helped herself to garlic bread. 'So . . . Leo . . . I see you've started lunch without us. You young people and your appetites, I don't know!'

'We were starving, Granny,' Sean protested. 'We've been waiting ages for you!'

Granny eyed my brother with amusement. 'Well, at least you weren't allowed to starve for *too* long, Sean.' She turned back to Leo. 'I must say it's good to know that you're experienced when it comes to dealing with children, Leo. Though I should think it must be extremely difficult to keep discipline when you're so close to your pupils in age, mustn't it?'

I gaped at her. What was she trying to do?

'Um, well, I don't think that's really a problem, thank goodness,' Leo said with a forced smile.

'Still . . . it's not an easy job, I'm sure. And I hear from Annabel that you don't get paid enough either.'

Leo immediately flushed bright red. 'Annabel said that?'

'Well, yes . . . of course it's probably an adequate salary for a young man like yourself with no responsibilities, but I must say that for a man with a family –'

'Mum only said that she doesn't think *teachers* get paid enough for the job they do,' I interrupted quickly. '*All* teachers, she meant.' I looked sternly at Granny to let her know that I could see exactly what she was up to.

Granny smiled sweetly, sat back in her chair, took her glasses out of her handbag and began to study the menu.

Just then a waiter brought a bottle of champagne over to our table. Mum was right behind him and she sat down with a smile as Granny raised her eyebrows at the sight of the bottle.

'I took the liberty of ordering it for us,' Mum explained.

'Oh, are we celebrating something?' Granny asked, looking for all the world like she genuinely didn't have a clue.

'Mother . . .' Mum's teeth were gritted and I think if the waiter hadn't been there she might have completely lost it.

'Ah, your engagement . . . *of course*! Sorry, my dear . . . a momentary lapse. No doubt you'll get them too when you're as old as me.' She looked straight at Leo as she added with a sugary smile, 'Of course for some of us that's still a very long way off.'

Thankfully the champagne seemed to relax the adults and the conversation got easier. Perhaps Granny relaxed a bit too much though, because as the waiter cleared away our plates (and Sean began to eye up the ice-cream machine, where you could go back for endless refills), she said with a wicked gleam in her eye, 'Leo, you do realise

152

Annabel is going to have grey hair and wrinkles whilst you're still a young man in your prime?'

The silence that followed was awful.

Then Leo put down his glass with a bit of a bang and said brightly, 'You know, I think it'll be fine so long as Annabel uses a good hair dye and doesn't hold back on the Botox!'

Mum looked shocked for a few moments and Granny looked totally gob-smacked. Then Mum burst out laughing, and that was when I first thought that maybe . . . just maybe . . . everything was going to work out all right after all.

'What time is your party finishing?' Sean asked me as the two of us walked back home after seeing Granny off on the train. Granny had managed to chisel in a few more awkward moments, but Leo had totally kept his cool. Mum and Leo had stayed behind to have coffee and a debrief at the station cafe.

'Eleven thirty. Raffy says ending it any earlier will look too pathetic.' I tried to sound confident, but Sean must have picked up on my nervousness.

'There's still time to cancel if you don't want to go through with it,' he said.

I gave him a *get-real* look. It was already half past three. Right now Lily and the girls would be at the pound shop buying supplies. It was way too late to cancel and he knew it.

Just then my phone started ringing.

'Mum, is everything OK?' I asked as I lifted it to my ear.

'Yes . . . but Leo and I have decided to take the train down to his parents' place this afternoon to tell them about our engagement. We'll see how it goes but we were thinking we might stay the night in a B&B and come back tomorrow since you're staying at Lily's tonight and Sean's staying at Zack's.'

This was the first I'd heard of my brother sleeping over at Zack's place, but then, like I said before, he doesn't always tell me everything these days. 'OK, Mum. Good luck!'

As I relayed the message to Sean, the news began to sink in and I started to grin. Now the coast was completely clear for us to hang out at Blossom House tonight! And I realised that part of the reason I'd been feeling so anxious all day was that I was worried Mum would somehow find out and stop it all happening.

Suddenly that threat was gone, and it felt like Lily and Raffy had been right all along. A party at Blossom House *was* the best idea ever!

Chapter Eighteen

As soon as I arrived at Blossom House that afternoon I felt happy. It was a beautiful spring day and the trees were still covered in blossom, though some petals had fallen and there was now a light pink scattering on the grass. The sky was blue, with only a few small clouds, and the sun was shining. I stood motionless for a few minutes listening to the birds tweeting, wondering if there were any babies in nests nearby.

'I love it here,' I actually said out loud.

I knew I had to go inside but I let myself stand there taking it all in for just a few moments longer. I couldn't believe that this would be my last spring here.

I'd brought my dress for the party with me so I went to hang it in the cupboard in the front bedroom. I would change into it later after the others got here. I thought briefly of Raffy and whether or not he would make any comment about my dress. Lily didn't much like vintage clothes, but that didn't mean that Raffy felt the same. I knew he loved to watch all the James Bond films, including the really early ones from the 1960s. The women in those films always looked dead glamorous, and I was guessing Raffy thought so too.

I glanced at my phone to check the time. I had half an hour before the others were due to get here with all the provisions for the party. I still couldn't quite believe what I was about to let happen, but then again our precious second home would soon be gone in any case. And knowing that, maybe it wasn't such a mad idea to throw this party. Yes, it would put an end to our personal private sanctuary once and for all . . . but that might make it easier to say goodbye to Blossom House for good when the time came.

Two hours later the massive front room was lit up with fairy lights and Raffy was yelling at Lily to get rid of them, saying they made the place look like 'some girlie fairy grotto'. Clara was emptying crisps and sweets into two big bowls and arguing with Lily about where to place them because there were no tables in the room and the only useable surfaces were the window ledge and the mantelpiece. Hanna was setting out paper cups and big bottles of fizzy drinks in the kitchen.

Soon everyone was arguing about whose iPod should go in the docking station first and I started panicking when I heard a vehicle with a siren passing by somewhere outside. For a minute I stood there imagining police cars screeching into the driveway and furious neighbours standing on the pavement shaking their fists at us as we were led out in handcuffs.

'Sasha, what are you doing? You're not even changed yet!' Lily scolded. Needless to say, Lily looked stunning in a mini skirt and strappy top combination that made her look about eighteen.

I knew I had to calm down and get myself upstairs pronto if I was going to be ready in my own dress by the time our first guests made an appearance.

Ellie, who was coming separately from the others, arrived while I was still getting changed. She'd promised to help me with my hair and make-up, and she immediately came to find me upstairs.

'Wow, Ellie!' I gasped when I saw her. She looked fantastic in a funky red and orange skirt and a gold top, her hair all spiky and sprayed with gold glitter.

157

'Wow yourself!' Ellie exclaimed. 'That dress is amazing on you, Sasha!'

'Thanks,' I said proudly. I really did love the dress. The black velvet bodice made it sophisticated while the fuchsia-pink skirt made it fun.

'That is definitely *not* a quiet dress,' Ellie told me with a grin as she came over to touch the overskirt of bead-studded black netting. 'And I definitely don't think you should have a quiet hair style.' She reached into her bag and pulled out a spray can of bright pink hair colour.

I gulped. 'Really?'

'Trust me. It's going to look great.'

First she helped me with my make-up. Then she put up my hair in a loose bun with lots of wispy bits coming down, sprayed the bun part completely pink and added some sparkly hair decorations.

Just as she was finishing off, Rafferty walked in on us. He stopped in his tracks and actually wolf-whistled when he saw me. 'You certainly scrub up a whole lot better than my little sister! Way to go, Sasha!'

I blushed furiously, half with pleasure, half with embarrassment. And I couldn't think of anything to say. I reminded myself that Raffy was fifteen and there was no way he could be interested in me. But maybe he'd wait a year or two. He'd definitely stopped thinking of me as a little kid, hadn't he?

'Haven't you heard of knocking? Girls are trying to get ready in here,' Ellie snapped at him.

'*Oops!* Sorry! Just came to tell you Priti's downstairs,' Raffy said with a grin. 'Says Sasha invited her. She looks . . . well . . . nothing like *she* looks at school either. Though she hasn't got pink hair.'

'Seriously wow!' Ellie murmured as she followed Rafferty out on to the landing.

I thought for a moment that she was commenting on Raffy's bum as he jogged down the stairs in front of us. Then I spotted Priti standing at the bottom of the staircase.

'Priti!' I exclaimed in delight. My friend looked absolutely stunning in the shimmering red 1950s dress. She had an orange silk shawl tied loosely round her shoulders and her black hair fell in glossy waves down her back.

Lily, Hanna and Clara were all standing in the hall gawping at her as if they'd just seen Cinderella.

'Priti!' I said as I reached the bottom of the stairs and gave her an excited hug. 'You look fantastic!'

'Priti, no way is that *you*!' Lily finally blurted.

'Thanks,' Priti murmured good-naturedly.

'Cool vintage dresses, girls!' Hanna exclaimed, giving us both a thumbs up.

'Yes,' agreed Lily. 'Very retro!'

Only Clara couldn't bring herself to say anything nice it seemed, though at least for once she refrained from saying anything nasty.

'In here, people,' Raffy announced, holding open the door to the front room, where he had already started the music, and I felt a nervous flutter in my tummy as we followed him inside.

He came to stand next to me while the others crowded round the snacks. 'Look, Sasha, I just wanted to say . . .'

I turned round to face him and suddenly he was looking straight into my eyes. I was conscious of my bare shoulders and I imagined him putting his arm round me. *Stop it, Sasha. It will never happen.*

'. . . thanks for letting us have this place. Lily told me you're a bit nervous because it's your first proper party, but you can relax now. I'll make sure nothing bad happens. Your mum will never know we were here.' He smiled and the light green flecks in his brown eyes seemed to shine. And as he walked away his hand touched my arm very briefly. I actually felt like I had stopped breathing for a few moments.

All this and the party had barely even started. I swallowed hard over the knot in my throat. Now all we had to do was wait for everyone else to arrive.

By nine o'clock the music was blaring out pretty loudly, although nobody was dancing. All of the snacks and drinks we'd bought had rapidly been consumed and I was a bit worried because a few of the older kids were drinking bottles of beer they'd brought with them.

To be honest, I wasn't enjoying myself as much as I'd expected. Weirdly enough, Priti looked like she was having a better time than me, chiefly because she seemed to be getting on really well with Ellie. Before, I'd been a bit concerned about Priti not fitting in with the others, but from the way those two had been completely absorbed in a conversation about henna tattoos for the last twenty minutes, I realised I needn't have worried.

Twenty minutes before Priti was due to meet her dad outside my place, she went upstairs to change back into her normal clothes.

'Mum might be home when I get back and she'll ask loads of questions if she sees this dress,' she explained as she handed it back to me. 'Talk about a dress making you feel like a princess,' she added wistfully as she pulled her hair back into its usual ponytail.

I half wished I could go with her but I knew I couldn't leave Blossom House until everyone else had gone. I'd already been upstairs with Lily twice to get people down from the empty rooms up there, and there was nothing I could do about the fact that a lot of the older kids were crammed into the back sitting room, which I'd wanted to keep off limits.

But the worst thing of all was that from the moment Raffy's friends had arrived he had acted like he hardly even knew me. I mean, I got the fact that he couldn't be seen hanging out with his kid sister's friend. I really did. But I'd hoped he might have found another moment to catch me on my own to ask me how I was doing.

After I'd seen Priti out I stopped to fill up a paper cup with water from the kitchen tap.

'Hi, Sasha,' said a familiar voice behind me.

I whirled round and saw Zack standing at the back door. He was wearing jeans and a blue T-shirt with a quirky cartoon of Bugs Bunny on the front and 'What's Up, Doc?' written on the back.

'What are *you* doing here?' I asked him in surprise.

'Mum and Dad have gone out and my big sister's in charge, so it was much easier to get away than I thought.' He paused. 'Wow, you look . . . *different*. I really like that dress. It suits you.'

'Thanks.'

Just then Sean walked in through the door behind Zack. He immediately pointed at my pink hair and fell about laughing.

'Shut up,' I snapped, though of course that wasn't going to stop him.

'At least there's not as much noise outside as I thought there'd be,' Sean said once he'd pulled himself together. 'You can't hear much at all from the street.'

'Told you it would be fine,' I snapped.

'Well, I don't know about fine!' He paused. 'You do realise Raffy's got *you* taking all the risk for a party that's full of *his* friends, don't you?'

'So?'

'Sasha, are you in here?' Lily came to the door of the kitchen and looked relieved when she found me.

'What is it, Lily?'

'Someone just told me that a crowd of Year Tens are mucking about in that old shed in the garden. Should we go and check it out, do you think? I can get Raffy to come with us.'

'If he's not *one* of them,' Sean muttered.

'It's OK, Lily, we'll go and check it out,' I told her, going over to the open back door where, when I looked out, I could make out movement at the end of the garden.

It was getting dark outside as Sean, Zack and I made our way across the grass and through the trees until we reached the spot where the trees ended and the wild part of the garden began. I stopped abruptly because I really didn't want to ruin my dress by carrying on through all the overgrown grass and brambles.

A friend of Raffy's called Jake and a few other Year Ten boys were gathered in front of the shed, standing round the big metal trunk, which they must have dragged outside. The box was open and they were shining their torches inside it, talking in low excited voices.

As I stared at them I realised some of them had obviously been drinking. What if we couldn't get them to leave at eleven thirty? I recognised Dylan Gibbs and Rajan Singh, who are both massive and play on the Helensfield High rugby team. Sean and Zack and I would be no match for them. Even Raffy wouldn't be able to force them to leave if they didn't want to.

'Hey, what are you doing with that?' Sean demanded as he approached them, seemingly completely oblivious to the need for caution.

All of the boys turned and pointed their torches at him.

'Hate to break this to you, guys, but those are torches, not guns!' my brother quipped.

There was a moment of silence before Dylan stepped forward and grabbed my brother roughly by the arm. 'Sean! Come and check this out, you idiot!'

Clearly Dylan and my brother knew each other pretty well and once again I found myself grudgingly admiring Sean's easy popularity. Soon Sean had all the older boys listening to him as he recounted how the man who used to live here had been a magician and how we thought the trunk had probably been his.

'Hey, I saw something on TV the other day about this magician called Houdini who was an amazing escape artist,' Jake piped up. 'This guy could escape from trunks like this that had padlocks on them and chains round them and everything!'

That's when Sean boasted, 'I bet *I* could do that too! My grandfather was a magician, you know. I reckon that kind of talent runs in families.'

Everybody groaned. 'Yeah . . . right, Sean.'

'If you want a go I think I've got a padlock on my bike that would fit this box!' Dylan teased.

'Sure! I bet I can escape from there in less than three minutes!' Sean declared, urging Dylan to go and fetch it.

'Sean, don't be stupid!' I snapped as Dylan went off.

'It's OK, Sasha.' Sean came over to me and whispered, 'A good kick from the inside and those rusty hinges will come right off. I can't wait to see their faces when I spring out of there!'

'But, Sean . . .' I trailed off. It was true that those hinges were so rusted through that one kick probably *would* be enough to break them off. But still . . .

Sean was already stepping into the trunk.

'Sean sure likes to show off, doesn't he?' Zack murmured as Rafferty appeared outside, along with Lily and several other people who had heard that something was going on in the garden.

'He likes to entertain people,' I murmured with a resigned sigh. Suddenly it struck me that clearly Sean *had* inherited something from our magician grandfather.

Sean lay down on his back inside the metal box, his knees drawn up in front of him, telling the others to go ahead and shut him in. I looked across at Raffy and noticed that a Year Ten girl called Sophie was leaning against him. As they stood there together, he stretched out his arm and curled it round her shoulder. I looked away really quickly, trying not to think about what I'd seen.

Dylan soon came back with the padlock and showed us that he had the key hanging safely on a chain round his neck. Then everyone went silent as the lid of the box went down and the padlock was clicked in place.

'GO!' yelled Rajan, who was timing it.

I sneaked a glance over at Raffy again. Sophie was snuggling up to him like she was his girlfriend. My heart was pounding and I just wanted to run away somewhere and hide. How could I ever have imagined myself as more than sensible Sasha, his kid sister's dorky best friend?

A steady thumping started up from inside the box as my brother began to kick repeatedly against the lid. Not very Houdini-like, I thought. A whole minute passed, then a second minute. The hinges on the trunk still held. In the rapidly fading light Lily got out her phone and shone the torch on the box as Sean kicked over and over again in the same spot. He was kicking so hard that we could actually see the metal lid getting dented.

After another minute the banging stopped and we heard Sean call out, 'If you guys are sitting on the lid, can you get off, please?'

'No one's sitting on the lid, Sean,' Rajan shouted back.

'Have you had enough? Shall we unlock it for you?' yelled Dylan.

There was a brief silence and then the kicking started up again. I couldn't understand how the hinges were still holding.

After a while Sean stopped again and sounded a bit breathless as he said, 'OK, I give in. Let me out, will you?'

'Not until we hear a *please*!' joked someone.

'Please,' Sean said, in a way that made me think he had definitely had enough.

Raffy came forward to help (Sophie had melted into the crowd) and we all watched as the padlock was removed. I was more than ready to start teasing my brother along with everybody else the second the lid came up. But then it became clear that that wasn't going to happen. Somehow the lid seemed to have got jammed.

'I can't shift it,' Dylan murmured, standing back to let someone else have a go.

'Guys, can you please hurry up?' came Sean's muffled voice from inside. He sounded a bit panicky as he added, 'It's hot in here and I could really use some air.'

'We're trying, Sean,' Raffy called out as he attempted in vain to budge the lid himself. 'The latch is jammed or something.'

And the worst thing of all was that Raffy actually sounded worried.

Chapter Nineteen

'Sasha, do you know if there are any tools here?' Raffy suddenly asked as I tried not to think about my brother being trapped inside that sealed metal box with no air holes.

'There are some under the stairs.'

'Can you go and get them?'

Zack came with me to fetch the tools from the house and we rushed back out to the garden with them, just as we heard Lily's voice yelling out, 'Hurry up! He's really starting to panic.'

Everybody stood back as I tipped the contents of the bag on to the ground and Raffy picked up a big sturdy screwdriver.

'Don't worry, Sean,' I called out to him. 'Raffy's going to unjam the latch.'

But it didn't turn out to be that easy as everyone with

a torch on his or her phone, shone it on to the box to give Raffy as much light as possible to work by.

'Sasha, I think it's time we phoned for help,' Zack said when five minutes had passed and Raffy still hadn't managed to get into the trunk.

'OK, but who?'

'The fire brigade maybe?'

'OK.' I was fighting down panic as I fumbled to get my phone out of my pocket, unable to stop my hands from shaking.

That's when we heard someone yelling at us from the direction of the house: 'WHAT'S GOING ON HERE?'

'Isn't that *Mr Anderson?*' I heard someone say as I looked up to see Leo making his way across the garden towards us.

'It *is* Mr Anderson!' someone confirmed, and suddenly Sean's predicament was temporarily forgotten as almost everybody scrambled to escape, horrified at the prospect of being caught here by a teacher.

'Sasha, is that *you?*' Leo was striding towards us through the trees and fleeing kids, sounding like he couldn't believe what he was seeing. He put up his arm to shield his eyes as a couple of people who had stayed to help shone their torches right in his face.

'Leo!' I called out, hugely relieved, and if anyone was surprised to hear me calling our teacher by his first name, then they didn't comment. 'Sean is trapped inside that box. It isn't locked but we can't get the lid off. It's like the latch has jammed or something.'

As if on cue Sean started yelling and banging hysterically on the lid.

'How long has he been in there?' Leo asked us tensely as he squatted down to inspect the latch for himself.

We told him and if anything he seemed relieved that it hadn't been longer.

'SEAN! IT'S LEO!' he shouted to get my brother's attention.

'Listen, we're going to get you out of there! But I need you to stop panicking and take some nice slow breaths. OK?'

'OK.' Sean's voice was hoarse but he did sound slightly calmer.

'Good boy. Now cover your ears. The next part is going to be noisy.'

It was all a bit of a blur after that.

After several more minutes of trying unsuccessfully to break off either the latch or the hinges Leo stopped and took Lily's torch from her, shining it on to the lid just above the latch. 'Did Sean make that dent there, do you think?' he asked as he peered at the metal more closely.

'I think so,' I said. 'He was kicking at it really hard.'

Leo frowned. 'I think maybe the top part of the latch has shifted out of alignment with the bottom part and that's what's caused it to jam. I'm going to try and straighten out this dent and see if that makes a difference.'

We watched as he carefully bashed at the dented part of the lid, then applied the screwdriver to the latch again. This time, after a bit of careful jiggling and a bit of brute force the two parts separated. As the lid came up, everyone cheered.

I rushed over to the box. 'Sean, are you OK?'

I could see straight away that he wasn't. His face was red and tear-streaked and his hair, damp with sweat, was standing on end. His body was trembling all over and it was clear that he was still in panic mode.

'Just take it easy, Sean. Stand up slowly,' Leo cautioned, but Sean wasn't listening. He was almost hysterical in his panic to get out of the box and he batted Leo's outstretched hand away and jumped out, only to have his knees buckle under him as soon as his feet touched the ground.

Leo caught him just before he fell and my brother didn't put up any resistance as Leo scooped him up and carried him into the house.

Most of the Year Tens had gone by the time we all got back inside. The few stragglers went without a fuss as soon as they realised Leo was there. Lily, Rafferty, Ellie and Zack all stayed behind after everyone else had left. When Leo saw them still hovering he told them to phone their parents and get themselves lifts home. Meanwhile, he sent me to go and wait with Sean while he did a sweep of the house and garden to check nobody else was still there.

I found my brother lying on the sofa in the front room, where Leo had taken him to calm down. He was still looking pretty shaken up. I was so grateful he was safe that a big part of me just wanted to run over and give him a massive hug.

'Ow!' Sean cried out when I marched over and whacked him really hard on the shoulder instead. 'What was *that* for?'

'Zack's right! You *do* just like showing off. I thought you were going to suffocate in there . . .' I didn't bother trying to explain how scared I'd been or how helpless I'd felt. I think I'd have started crying if I'd said any more right then.

Sean obviously got the message because, for once, he didn't try and joke his way out of it.

We were sitting quietly side by side on the sofa when Leo came back into the room. We'd heard him handing our friends over to their parents and we knew we weren't the only ones in big trouble.

'Where's Mum?' I asked him in a small voice.

'At home.'

Sean said nervously, 'We thought you guys weren't coming back until tomorrow.'

'No kidding?' Leo glared at him before explaining, 'We decided we may as well get the last train back tonight, and on the way your mum got a call from Miranda asking her to check that everything was OK at Blossom House. One of the neighbours had phoned saying he thought he'd heard some kids in the garden. Your mum was exhausted when we got back though, so I took her home and said I'd check it out.' He shook his head at us. 'Have you seen your face, Sasha? Go and wash off that make-up. And you'd better hope that pink stuff comes out of your hair.' He turned to Sean, the tension in his voice going up a notch. 'As for *you* . . . what the hell were you thinking just now?'

'Well . . .' My brother attempted to make light of it. 'I thought I could do the whole Houdini thing . . . you know . . .'

'No, Sean, I *don't* know.'

'Oh, well . . . Houdini was that guy who –'

'I know who Houdini *was*, thank you!' Leo snapped.

'Oh, right . . . well, it was supposed to be a joke, you see . . . showing them I could escape from the box. I really thought the hinges would break off when I kicked the lid and I could jump out and shout, "Ta-dah!"' He threw out his hands in a *ta-dah* sort of gesture.

Leo just glared at him. 'You think this is funny?'

'Well, I think if it had gone according to plan then it *could* have been . . .' Sean stopped abruptly when he saw the look Leo was giving him. 'Or *not*,' he added self-consciously.

'Nobody else is laughing, Sean,' Leo said through gritted teeth. 'Not your sister. Not your friends. And certainly not *me*!'

'Listen . . .' Sean began, nervously licking his lips.

'No, Sean, *you* listen! You could have been seriously hurt pulling a stunt like that! Maybe you get a kick out of taking risks, or maybe you just haven't learnt to think before you act, but either way it has got to stop! Do you hear me?'

Sean didn't reply.

'I SAID, DO YOU HEAR ME?' Leo bawled.

Sean jumped slightly and he suddenly looked really young as he managed to rasp, 'Yes, Leo.'

'And what's more I can't *believe* you decided to throw a party here! I mean, your mother could lose her job over this!'

'But the party wasn't –' my brother began, but Leo wouldn't let him speak.

'I expected better from you, I really did! But I guess I was wrong to think you were becoming more responsible. You obviously can't be trusted. In fact, since you seem to have all the maturity of a five-year-old, maybe *that's* how we need to treat you from now on!'

I opened my mouth to speak but Leo was already storming out of the room.

'It's OK, Sean. I'll tell him the party was my idea!' I said, feeling terrible.

My brother turned his face into the sofa. 'Why bother?' he hissed in a choked voice. 'As far as he's concerned, *I'm* the bad kid in this family!'

And although his face was hidden I was pretty sure he was crying.

Chapter Twenty

Sean was the one who woke me up the following morning and straight away I heard raised voices coming from downstairs.

Mum and Leo were arguing. The thing was, Mum and Leo never argued. If Mum ever started to, Leo would stay calm and refuse to rise to the bait.

'Jeez!' I said as I swung my legs round to sit on the edge of my bed.

'I know. That's why I thought I should wake you up.'

'Do you think we should go downstairs?'

'I think *you* should. *I'm* the one they're arguing about. Leo doesn't think Mum gives me enough boundaries apparently.'

'You've been listening?'

'It's been hard not to. Leo's been going on and on about how he can't believe I threw that party.'

I started to pull on my fleece over my pyjamas. 'But I told them last night that the party was my idea.'

Mum had bawled out Sean and me big time when Leo had brought us home. She was so mad she even said something I'd never heard her say before: 'I'm utterly ashamed of you! And if your dad was alive, he'd be ashamed of you too!'

That's when we knew it was really bad. Mum didn't talk much about our dad these days, but when things were good – when I did well at school, or when Sean took a particularly brilliant photograph – she'd hug us and say, 'Your dad would be so proud of you.' And her eyes would brim and we'd feel a little bit awkward, but happy at the same time. This was the exact opposite. I felt terrible, and Sean must have been feeling even worse.

'Yeah, well, Leo thinks you're covering for me,' Sean informed me now. 'He just told Mum he thinks you act more like a mother hen to me than a sibling. *Inappropriately protective*, I think he said.'

'That's just dumb!' I protested. 'Sean, come downstairs with me. I'll explain again how the party was my idea and –'

'No, it doesn't matter any more.'

'Of course it matters! We have to sort this out!'

'No, we don't! I know now what he really thinks of me and –'

He broke off as we heard the front door slam.

We both looked at each other in alarm and I ran to look out of the window. I saw that it was Mum who had just left the house.

Seconds later we heard footsteps on the stairs.

'Leo,' I mumbled nervously as he came into my room.

'Good morning, Sasha,' he said crisply, like he didn't think it was a good one at all, before turning to my brother, who was sitting down on the end of my bed. 'Sean.'

'Where's Mum gone?' Sean grunted.

'To inspect the mess you made last night. She's already spoken to Lily's mother. Lily and Rafferty are going to meet you at Blossom House in half an hour to help you clean up – preferably before Miranda sees the place. You two had better get dressed.'

'Right,' I murmured. As Leo started to leave my room, I said, 'Leo, the party last night . . . it honestly was all my idea. Sean had nothing to do with it. He only came there to check I was OK.'

Leo let out a hollow laugh. 'Really? He thought he'd keep an eye on you from inside that airtight box, did he?'

And before either of us could respond, he had whizzed off down the stairs saying that he was going to get on with some marking.

When Sean left I got dressed carefully in a strappy sequinned top and my jeans with the designer label that Mum had picked up for me in a charity shop (and which Lily says are much cooler than the jeans I usually wear). At the last minute I decided to put on some make-up as well.

I had just gone downstairs and was grabbing a handful of biscuits to eat for breakfast when Leo came into the kitchen.

His gaze moved disapprovingly over my jeans and strappy top and settled on my face. 'Sasha, I thought you were going to Blossom House to clean up?'

'I am!'

'Then why are you dressed like you're going to another party? And you're only twelve years old, for God's sake! Is it really necessary to smother your face with all that muck?'

I felt my face go hot. OK, so I might have gone a bit heavy on the foundation but there was no way I looked that bad. I started to feel cross.

Sean didn't help by appearing in the kitchen and saying, 'Of course it's necessary. *Raffy* will be there!'

Leo looked puzzled as I yelled at my brother to shut up.

'Raffy?' Leo repeated. 'But isn't he –'

'Nearly three years older than her and a total numb-skull!' Sean declared. 'That's right! Doesn't stop her having a massive crush on him though!'

'Shut up, Sean!' I yelled more savagely. My face felt like it was on fire. How long had he known?

'Sasha, I really think you should change into something more sensible,' Leo said, while looking as if he was trying to work out if what my brother had just said was true.

I'm not sure what came over me next. It felt like some furious cranky girl, whose existence I had only been vaguely aware of before then, suddenly exploded out from inside me and bawled, 'GET LOST, LEO!'

And I stormed out of the house in a total rage, slamming the front door as hard as I could behind me.

I half-ran, half-hobbled, all the way to Lily's house, crying a little on the way, hoping they hadn't left for Blossom House yet. (On top of everything else, the toe strap on one of my flip-flops had become loose and it was proving difficult to keep on.)

'I HATE HIM!' I burst out the second Lily opened her front door.

'Who?' she asked, looking surprised.

'LEO!'

I hadn't meant to blurt everything out so dramatically, but I just couldn't help it. As we stood on her front doorstep I gave her a blow-by-blow account of what had just happened, leaving out the embarrassing bits about her brother.

'You'll just have to tell Leo you need more time to adjust before he starts going all overprotective dad on you,' Lily advised me after she had listened.

I sniffed. 'You think that's what he's doing?'

'Sounds like it. And I don't blame you for not wanting to take it. After all, he's not even married to your mum yet! He's lucky you didn't ... I don't know ...' She glanced down at my feet. 'Throw your flip-flops at him or something!'

I smiled briefly, imagining the look on his face if I had.

'Never mind – you can save that for the next time!' Lily added mischievously.

'Next time?'

'Trust me, this isn't the only time he's going to try and tell you what to do ... at least if he's anything like *my* dad.' She grinned. 'Once I got so mad at mine I threw a yoghurt at him. I've never actually walked out of the house on him though. I probably wouldn't see my phone for a month if I did that.'

'You reckon?' I suddenly worried that my outburst was going to have consequences – on top of the ones I knew would soon be coming my way as a result of the party, that is. I quickly realised it might be smart to get Mum on my side sooner rather than later.

'Don't worry. *Your* mum won't do anything like that. She's way too cool,' Lily said, like she could read my mind.

'Yeah, well Leo certainly *isn't* cool,' I grumbled. 'I mean, out of Mum and him . . . well, it's almost like *he's* the one who's nearly forty and *she's* the one who's nine years younger!'

Lily was grinning.

'What's so funny?' I demanded.

'*You!* I just can't believe you yelled at Mr Anderson like that. Hey, don't look offended! I think the new rebellious you is awesome. And *I* think you look great . . . even if you do look like you're going out on a date!'

When Lily and I arrived at Blossom House I quickly told Mum what had happened between Leo and me. I might have skewed the account a little in my favour, but I figured Leo could have phoned Mum and done the same, and that if he hadn't that was his problem.

'He's going against what *you* think about Sasha's clothes,' Lily backed me up. 'I mean, you're her mum and if you didn't want her wearing those designer jeans then you wouldn't have bought them for her, would you?'

Mum just glared at her. Clearly she was still very cross with us about the party.

'Actually, Lily, I totally agree with him that dressing up just to come here to clean does seem rather pointless. Now . . . you'd better make a start on the garden. Where are the boys by the way?'

'Sean's just coming,' I said.

'Raffy's coming a bit later,' Lily mumbled, avoiding looking Mum in the eye. She had already told me that her brother had conveniently disappeared soon after he'd been told he had to come and help us. I felt quite relieved. I wasn't sure I'd be able to talk to Raffy normally after seeing him with his arm round that other girl last night.

'Good, because Miranda is bringing her client round to view the place again with his partner first thing tomorrow morning,' Mum snapped. 'So I want it completely back to normal by then.'

'So it's not definite that he's going to buy it then?' I said. 'I mean, he could still change his mind?'

Mum narrowed her eyes at me as if she was trying to work out why I was so interested. But before she could ask Lily was picking up the roll of black bin bags Mum had left out for us and giving my arm an impatient tug. 'Come on, Sasha,' she urged.

And I have to say I was brought down to earth with a bump as I surveyed the garden and all the discarded rubbish from the night before.

Half an hour later the garden was tidy again and Lily and I had placed a couple of bin bags of rubbish with the other stuff waiting to be collected at the front entrance. I spotted the birdcage from the shed in the pile of stuff being thrown out and, acting on an impulse, I took it back inside the house with me and hid it in the bedroom cupboard.

I went back downstairs to find Sean and Lily about to make a start on cleaning up in the front room.

'You might need to use the vacuum cleaner in there first,' Mum was telling them as she stood in the hall handing out cloths and cleaning fluids.

'It's broken,' I said without thinking.

186

'What?' She whirled round to glare at me. 'Don't tell me *that* happened at your party?'

'Well . . . no, but . . .' I trailed off, looking at Sean, not sure what to say next.

The two of us had accidentally broken Blossom House's ancient-looking vacuum cleaner the December before. I'd been making my own Christmas cards there one Saturday while Mum was at work, and Sean had ended up helping me and getting really silly with the glitter. While I was vacuuming up the mess, a little tube of glue had somehow got sucked up into the hoover and we hadn't been able to get it to work ever since.

'Come on, Mum – it *has* to be broken!' Sean said, doing his best to rescue me. 'Have you *seen* that thing? It looks like it belongs in a museum for ancient household contraptions!'

And he quickly pushed me ahead of him into the front room before Mum could respond.

Needless to say the front room was a complete mess. There were paper cups everywhere, some empty and some with bits of drink still left in them. Sticky sweets and crisps were trodden into the polished wooden floor that I had once been so proud of. Thankfully nothing structural seemed to have been damaged. (I knew for a fact that the one crack in the windowpane had been there before the party.)

The fairy lights were still up, so Lily and I started to take them down.

'Yuck!' Lily exclaimed as she stood on a sticky blob of chewing gum.

'Maybe I should get the house professionally cleaned,' Mum said with a frown as she watched us. 'I don't want to risk losing my job over this.'

I remembered Leo saying Mum could lose her job because of what we'd done, but at the time I'd thought he was just sounding off. Plus he didn't know anything about Mum's boss Miranda. Hearing Mum say it made me think again. 'But this isn't your fault, Mum. Why would Miranda fire you?'

Mum was looking at me like I was incredibly stupid. 'Because you and Sean are minors. I'm responsible for what you do. Even Leo agrees. And Miranda's furious that I allowed this to happen.'

'Mum, I'm so sorry,' I blurted. 'I didn't think.'

Mum scowled. 'Well, that's what Leo and I find hard to understand, Sasha. You *always* think. I mean, this is completely out of character for you! Sean . . . *yes* . . . I can believe he would do something like this and not give any thought to the consequences – and then be very sorry about it afterwards. But not *you* . . .'

I felt my cheeks burning and my eyes prickling. I stared hard through the window at the cherry trees and tried not to cry. Mum completely ignored Sean's huffy snort of indignation and looked at me as if she expected some sort of response.

Lily gave a little cough. 'Actually it was Raffy and me who persuaded Sasha to let us have the party here,' she confessed.

But Mum shook her head. 'Sasha would never do anything she didn't agree with just because you suggested it, Lily. No . . . I'm afraid there has to be more to it than that. Leo thinks Sasha is covering for Sean but –'

Just then we heard new footsteps in the hall and a hesitant voice calling out, 'Hey, is anyone in here?'

'Raffy!' I gasped, standing up and self-consciously smoothing down my top, which had ridden up slightly while I was crouching down.

As he strolled into the room looking really cool and casual in jeans and a light blue sweatshirt, I could feel the familiar pink flush I always seemed to get in his presence start to creep up my face.

'Mum and Dad sent me,' he explained a bit sheepishly. 'Sorry I'm late.'

Mum was looking thoughtful as she turned her gaze away from Raffy and on to me. In fact, scrub thoughtful . . . As I kept blushing furiously, Mum was staring at me as if a gigantic light bulb had just switched itself on inside her head.

Chapter Twenty-One

It was an hour or so later, while Lily and I were on our own cleaning up in the back sitting room, that Lily found the photograph. She was sweeping the floor when the bristles on her brush must have nudged it out slightly from its position stuck between two floorboards. Lily knelt down and carefully pinched the protruding corner of the photo between finger and thumb.

'Look at this,' she said as she pulled it out. 'I guess it must have fallen out of an album or something when the house was being cleared. 'Oh wow!'

'What is it?'

'Well, isn't that the dress you were wearing at the party?'

'Let's see . . .' It certainly looked like the same dress, though because it was a black and white photograph it wasn't possible to tell the colours. The young woman wearing it seemed to be in her twenties or early thirties. She was very small and dainty-looking with a tiny waist and shoulder-length wavy hair. A young man dressed in a smart suit was standing with his arm round her shoulders. He looked very tall compared to her.

'There's something written on the back,' Lily said.

I turned it over and saw some words scribbled in black pen: *May 1955 – our engagement party*.

'I'm guessing this must be the old lady who lived here,' I said. 'I guess her son might want this photo. We should give it to Miranda.'

Mum came into the room then. 'Have you two nearly finished? Rafferty's done cleaning in the bathroom and I've said he can go home.'

'Mum, look what Lily just found stuck between the floorboards.'

'Let me see.' Mum took the photo and stared at it, shaking her head like she couldn't believe it.

'What is it, Mum?'

'It's just . . . well . . . this looks just like a picture I've got of my father when he was a young man. In fact I could swear this man *is* my father.'

'Well, he can't be, Mum,' I said dismissively. 'That's got to be the old lady who used to live here because she's wearing one of those dresses from the wardrobe upstairs.'

But instead of letting it drop, Mum stared at the photograph for ages, shaking her head and looking really puzzled.

The brilliant thing was, this photograph seemed to have distracted Mum from her anger with us. As soon as we got home she phoned Granny to tell her about it. But apparently Granny was very dismissive when Mum told her about the man in the photograph looking uncannily like our grandfather.

'She was *too* dismissive,' Mum told us when she got off the phone. 'I just have this feeling that she knows something she's not letting on. And when I think about it, she acted quite strangely when I showed her round Blossom House the other day . . .'

'Mum, Granny *always* acts strangely,' joked Sean.

Mum gave him a sharp look. 'I'd watch the smart mouth if I were you, young man. Don't forget you are in serious trouble.' She put the photo away in her bag and didn't say any more about it.

Normally I'd have been falling over myself to solve any potential mystery involving Blossom House – but right now I had some other things I needed to sort out first.

Most importantly, I had to speak to Leo again about the party.

'So you see the party really *was* my idea, not Sean's,' I told him that evening. 'Sean thought it was a bad idea from the start and he even tried to talk me out of it, but I wouldn't listen. I'm so sorry, Leo.'

I knew Mum had already had a quiet word with Leo about how she thought I'd gone along with the whole party idea to impress Rafferty. Plus I was sure Leo must have told Mum what Sean had said earlier about my so-called 'massive crush' on him.

I only hoped Leo didn't want to talk to me directly about my feelings for my best friend's brother, because I was pretty sure I'd die of embarrassment if he did.

Leo nodded at me. 'OK, Sasha. I'll go and speak to Sean. But you're both in a lot of trouble. You realise that?'

I did. Plus I knew I still had to apologise for yelling at him so nastily when I'd left the house earlier.

But before I could, he beat me to it.

'Listen, Sasha . . . about this morning . . . I'm sorry if I overreacted a bit about what you were wearing.' He paused. 'The trouble is, even though I'm not officially part of this family yet . . . well, I guess I can't help feeling a bit protective of you . . .'

'Oh, that's what Lily said!' I blurted before I could stop myself. I must say, I felt rather touched by his admission, until I got a sudden image of being shut up in some tower like Rapunzel for the rest of my life, just so he could make sure I didn't run off with any dodgy princes. 'Still, there's protective and *over*protective,' I pointed out firmly.

'Oh, I know that, Sasha.' He was struggling not to smile. 'Don't worry. I'll try and get the balance right in future. Remember I'm new to this though. You might have to bear with me for a little while.'

Mum came into the room then. 'Listen, Sasha,' she said briskly. 'As a punishment for the party I'm stopping your allowance for the next couple of months – Sean's too of course. I'm also taking away all your electronics, from both of you, for the next fortnight. That means no phones, no iPods, no Xbox and no using the laptop for anything other than schoolwork. And you can both write letters of apology to Miranda.'

I nodded solemnly to show that I accepted the punishment. 'Though it's not really fair on Sean,' I pointed out. 'He's got way more electronic stuff than me.'

'Well, that's too bad,' Mum said impatiently. 'And stop standing up for your brother all the time, Sasha! He *can* speak for himself, you know.'

I suddenly wondered if some of what Leo had said while they were rowing that morning had affected her after all.

As I left the room I heard Mum murmur, 'She looks every bit the teenager in that get-up, doesn't she?' She let out a weary sigh. 'If she's anything like *I* was in my teens, it's going to be buckle-your-seat-belts time in this house pretty soon.'

I almost felt like going back to reassure her that no way was I going to be *anything* like her as a teenager. I've heard all the stories about Mum's teenage years, and frankly I can't imagine getting up to even *half* the stuff that she did.

In the end though, I decided to let things be. After all, if Mum wanted to worry about me turning out to be just like her, then who was I to stop her?

Chapter Twenty-Two

The next morning I was feeling very nervous about going back to school. I just knew everyone would be talking about the party. It was major gossip material, made worse by the fact that Leo was the one who had caught us. I couldn't help thinking how lucky it was that it had only been Leo (without Mum) who had caught us at Blossom House on Saturday night. If Mum had been with him, there'd have been no way to prevent their big secret coming out. At least now we could pretend it was pure coincidence that Leo happened to be passing. And since no one at school (apart from Lily) knew the truth about them, there was no reason for anyone to suspect anything different.

Leo left for school before us with strict instructions to both of us not to be late. Why, oh, why did we have to have Leo as our registration teacher this week of all weeks?

As we ate breakfast, Sean suddenly clutched his stomach and complained that he felt sick. If you ask me, he was just feeling nervous too, though Mum immediately started flapping and telling him to get up to the bathroom because she didn't want him throwing up all over the table. (He did that once when he was younger and Mum's never forgotten it.)

Since she didn't go upstairs with him, Mum couldn't really argue when he came down five minutes later and reported that he'd been sick in the loo. She told him to go to his room to rest and ignored my disbelieving face as she phoned the school to say he wouldn't be in.

And not for the first time I wished Mum wouldn't be quite so amenable every time Sean decided that he needed the day off.

The trouble started as I crossed the playground just after the bell had rung. Becky Addams, a Year Ten girl I hardly knew, came and stood in front of me. Her mates were quick to follow.

'Hey, Sasha! Is it true your mum's shacking up with Mr Anderson?' she asked.

'What?' My voice came out so hoarse that even I could hardly hear it.

'Come on, Sasha! You can stop pretending. Everybody knows!'

I was starting to feel really light-headed as they fired questions at me:

'So how long have they been together?'

'Come on, Sasha! We want to hear all the juicy bits!'

'Yeah, Sasha! *Dish!*'

'So have you seen him in his pyjamas?'

'Does he snore?'

'Does he actually *wear* pyjamas?'

'How do you ever get to sleep at night knowing he's in the same house as you?'

'Does he work out?'

'My mum says he's got to be about *half* your mum's age! Is that true?'

'Yes, Sasha . . . is it even *legal* for them to be together?'

They all laughed and I tried not to let them see how humiliated I was. How did they know?

Just breathe: in and out . . . in and out . . . in and out . . .

I stood still as their voices swirled around me as a single mass of noise, muffled only by the loud thumping sound in my head as the blood pumped round it furiously.

I just couldn't get over the fact that they all *knew*. Because I was absolutely certain that nobody had known on Saturday night. I thought really hard. I knew I'd called Leo by his first name while Sean was trapped in that box, but nobody had commented at the time and I was pretty certain no one had noticed. Had I got that wrong? Or had there been some other clue that he was more than just a teacher to us?

As they all carried on laughing, I walked away, wishing I didn't feel so helpless and alone. If only Sean was with me . . . or, better still, Lily.

In fact where *was* Lily? Normally I'd see her in the playground at around this time. And if she saw me being picked on she'd be the first one to rush over to back me up. Today, however, there was no sign of her, or any of her pals.

My legs felt wooden as I somehow forced them to carry me into the school building towards my registration room. Oh, God, did *Leo* realise that everyone knew? Would anyone in our registration class say anything? Some other kids were giggling and whispering as they walked past me. Were they talking about Leo and Mum? How was I *ever* going to get through a whole day of this?

Just then I saw Clara and Hanna. When they spotted me they both started grinning.

'Hey, Sasha,' Clara greeted me. 'Listen, I know Lily says it's no big deal about your mum and Mr Anderson. But you know what?' She paused dramatically. 'It really, really *is*!'

Hanna started giggling then.

I froze. '*Lily* told you it's no big deal?'

'Yeah . . . well, Lily always has a soft spot for you underdog types!'

'Get lost, Clara!' I snapped, while in my head one word was repeating itself over and over: *Lily, Lily, Lily* . . .

Lily had been the only one who knew about Leo and Mum!

And tears started to prick my eyes as I realised who must have given away our secret.

It was beginning to feel like the worst day of my life. Well, OK, not really. That was probably still the day my dad died, but at least on *that* day I'd been too young to fully understand at the time *just* how bad a day I was actually having. (I mean, I know *now* just how final a thing dying is, but back then, when the grown-ups told me he was gone, I kept on imagining him as kind of waiting in the wings somewhere rather than gone for good. Though seeing the bereavement counsellor helped me a bit with that, I suppose.)

I ended up avoiding registration and hiding out in the girls' toilets instead. I know it must sound daft, but I couldn't imagine feeling *more* shaky if someone had just told me Lily had been run over by a bus.

Come on, Sasha. Get a grip. Nobody died.

But Lily had still betrayed me, and that felt so huge that even focusing on my breathing didn't make me feel much steadier.

As soon as the bell rang to signal the end of registration I set off to find Leo in the English department office.

'Sasha, where have you been?' he asked in a concerned voice as I met up with him just outside the door. 'Is something wrong? Where's Sean?'

'Sean's OK,' I reassured him at once. 'He's off sick today.'

'Really?' Leo was frowning.

'It's nothing serious,' I added, knowing that my brother avoiding school was the least of our worries right now. 'Leo, I'm sorry but I couldn't face coming to registration.'

I lowered my voice to a whisper. 'People know about you and Mum.'

Leo actually swore – which is something he hardly ever does in front of us, and absolutely never does in school (well, not within earshot of any pupils, in any case).

'Sorry,' he apologised, going a bit pink as he added, 'I guess that explains all the sniggers I was getting in registration this morning.'

I swallowed over my dry throat. 'It was Lily who told them.'

'Lily? How did *she* know?'

'She's known for ages, Leo! She's my best friend. I couldn't keep it a secret from her.' I felt on the verge of tears again.

Leo must have clocked my distress because he immediately softened his tone. 'It's OK, Sasha. Your mum and I didn't mean to keep it a secret forever in any case. Perhaps it's just as well it's out in the open.' He put his hand on my shoulder and guided me out into the corridor, where other pupils were hurrying to their first lesson of the day. 'You'd better get going to your next class. We'll talk about this tonight. But, Sasha, now that it's out there, try and pretend like it's no big deal, OK? The less of a reaction people get from you, the quicker they'll stop teasing. This will be a five-minute wonder, you'll see. In a couple of weeks something else will be the new hot topic. We just have to hold our heads up in the playground – and in the staffroom – until then. Deal?'

I sniffed, feeling slightly better that the two of us were in this together. 'Leo, are you going to get into trouble about this?'

'Hey, don't you worry about me. Though I'd better go and speak to Mr Jamieson before he hears about it on the grapevine.' He pulled a bit of a pained face, which made me smile despite the direness of the situation. Sometimes I forget that our fearsome head teacher is Leo's boss and that Leo is just as keen to stay on the right side of him as we are.

As I headed for my first class, I groaned. It was PE and Lily, Clara and Hanna were all in the same class as me. Luckily, so was Priti, and I made up my mind to stick with her and try and ignore the others.

I was the last person to arrive in the changing room and only Priti and a couple of other girls were still there getting ready. Everyone else was outside warming up for cross-country running. (Basically that means jogging round the boundary of our school, through the little park next door, then back round the boundary again.)

As I greeted Priti it took me a few moments to realise she wasn't going to reply. I waited until we were the last two in the changing room before asking her outright what was wrong. She flounced her ponytail aggressively and said that if I didn't know, then she wasn't going to tell me.

I couldn't think what she was so cross about – unless she had heard about Mum and Leo and didn't approve for some reason. But why wouldn't she? Sure, there was the age difference, and the fact that Leo was my teacher, but why would she be upset about that? I shook my head, not understanding what the problem was at all.

'Come on, Sasha! Get a move on!' Mrs Delaney, our PE teacher, called out from the doorway. I didn't know if my teacher had heard about Mum and Leo yet, but in any case all the teachers would know soon enough, and then my humiliation would be complete. Maybe I could convince Mum to let me switch schools, I thought miserably. Or maybe I should copy Sean and pretend to be sick.

I was jogging on my own round the first corner – which is where all the slackers stop running and start walking and chatting to their mates – when I heard my name being called.

Lily was standing waiting for me – and not just Lily, but Clara and Hanna too. My heart was pounding away furiously.

'Sasha . . .' Lily began, looking nervous. 'Listen, I need to tell you something –'

I hadn't wanted to talk to her at all. If I could have avoided seeing Lily for the next ten years, I would have. But I didn't for one moment expect her to try to justify herself to me.

'A secret is a secret,' I interrupted her. 'You promised you wouldn't tell anybody, Lily! You *promised*! You're meant to be my best friend!'

'Sasha, I *am* your best friend but –'

'YOU'RE NOT!' I screamed, all the stress and tension of the last few days bursting out unchecked. 'FRIENDS DON'T DO WHAT YOU DID!' Then I ran on away from her, racing along the muddy track round the edge of our school, not stopping until I got a stitch in my side and Lily had been left far behind. Tears were streaming down my face and my nose was running. I wiped the whole lot with the front of my T-shirt.

Nobody was watching and, even if they were, I didn't much care.

I looked up and realised that Priti was just ahead of me, jogging steadily and not looking back. Don't ask me why, but I think she knew I was there.

I panted as I pushed myself to catch up with her.

'Priti, wait! Please tell me why you're so mad at me!' I gasped as I finally got close enough to talk.

Priti glared at me, looking very hot and very angry. 'Why didn't you tell me about your mum and Mr Anderson?'

'I couldn't, Priti. Mum made us promise –'

'You told *Lily*!' She had slowed to walking pace now.

'I know, but only because . . . because Lily . . .' I trailed off, suddenly seeing why she was so mad – and knowing there was nothing I could say at this point that wouldn't make things even worse.

'Don't worry! I get it! Lily's your best friend, not me! Still . . .' She let out an almost triumphant snort. 'It seems like you were wrong about being able to trust her, doesn't it?'

'Priti, I . . .'

I slowed down and let her go on ahead of me.

She was right of course. I *had* picked the wrong friend to trust. It had just seemed natural to tell Lily. I mean Lily had been my best friend for so long that I'd always felt like she knew all my secret stuff even *before* I told her.

Lily had changed, I decided. And it was Clara and the others who had done it. And I had been really blind not to see it.

Tears were welling up in my eyes again as I trudged round the remainder of the course. In just a few hours I had managed to become the most ridiculed person in school *and* lose both my best friends.

I had never felt so lonely.

Chapter Twenty-Three

For the first time ever Leo actually gave me a lift home
after school. I had waited behind in the school library
after most people had gone home because I wanted to
avoid everybody on the way out. Lunchtime had been
bad enough. Three people had asked me if I'd seen Leo in
his boxers, and Hanna and Clara just seemed to crease up
in giggles every time they looked at me. No way was I
letting myself in for any more of a grilling. Leo came into
the library to give back some books, saw me sitting there
on my own and immediately suggested we should head
off together.

'How was your day?' he asked me in the car.

'Terrible,' I replied. 'Yours?'

'Ditto. I ended up shouting at one of the other
teachers in the staffroom.'

'Really? Which one?'

'It doesn't matter – the point is it happened just as Mr Jamieson was walking in to get his morning dose of caffeine.'

'Oh no! What did he say?'

'He said, "Excuse me, children, is this the playground or the staffroom?"'

'Ouch!'

'*I* thought so. I started to explain and he told me to save my breath to cool my porridge. I thought he was going to call me "laddie" but I was spared that, thank God!'

'Oh, Leo!' I started to laugh.

We were driving back past the little row of shops near our school when we spotted Zack coming out of the pet shop.

'Zack is the only person who's acted normally towards me all day,' I told Leo. 'He kept me company at lunch-time, though I had to hear all about his pet tarantula. Apparently Tallulah is an excellent "starter spider" and just the kind of tarantula I should get if I ever fancy having one as a pet!'

Leo laughed until he looked in his rear-view mirror and saw my brother coming out of the pet shop behind Zack.

'I thought he was meant to be sick,' Leo murmured,

screeching into the nearest parking space and exiting the car in a matter of seconds.

I waited where I was and the next thing I knew Sean was climbing grumpily into the back seat as Leo slammed the door shut behind him.

Needless to say, Leo was furious, and after he'd pulled out on to the road again he demanded to know why Sean had taken the day off school if he was well enough to go out on a shopping trip with Zack.

'I felt better this afternoon. What's the big deal?' Sean protested, at which point Leo nearly crashed into the car in front, which had stopped at a pedestrian crossing.

We all stayed quiet after that.

As soon as Leo parked up outside our house, Sean leapt out of the car and rushed to the front door to let himself in. He went straight through to the kitchen and I quickly followed, seizing the opportunity to speak with him alone while Leo was still fetching in his stuff.

'Sean, what's going on?' I asked as I watched him fiddling around in the freezer and eventually taking out an ice lolly.

'I just didn't want to face everyone after that whole nightmare with the box on Saturday night. I felt ... I don't know ... a bit of an idiot.'

I was surprised. Sean almost never talks about his emotions, or admits to feeling embarrassed.

'I hate to tell you this,' I said slowly, 'but everyone's over that already. Lily told someone about Mum and Leo. Now the whole school knows, even the teachers. *That*'s what everyone's talking about.'

'Oh my God,' he said disbelievingly. 'I bet the whole school is loving that!'

'It's been awful,' I said. 'Even the Year Elevens have been giving me funny looks.'

Sean laughed. 'They'll get over it. You know all the girls have got massive crushes on Leo, don't you? They're probably dead jealous of Mum.' He frowned slightly. 'But listen, I'm surprised at Lily telling anyone. I didn't think she'd do that to you.'

'Neither did I.' I lowered my voice. 'Sean, what were you doing in the pet shop just now?'

'Tell you later. Right now I have to get upstairs and start being a good little sick boy again before Leo gets on my case.'

'Too late for that, Sean,' Leo said as he entered the kitchen behind us. 'But you can certainly go up to your room and make a start on all the homework I managed to procure for you.'

'*Homework?* Come on, Leo, give it a break, can't you? I mean, don't tell me *you* never pulled a sickie when you were a kid!'

Leo looked surprised. 'Actually, Sean, I never did. Both my parents were teachers, remember. My life wouldn't have been worth living if I had, especially as my dad was best mates with my headmaster.'

'Oh yeah . . . I forgot . . . sorry.' Sean actually smiled. 'You know, that really explains a lot. Keep reminding me so I can make more allowances for you!'

And he disappeared upstairs with a cheeky grin on his face before Leo could respond.

Later that evening I walked in on Mum and Leo while they were discussing my brother in the kitchen. It wasn't a private discussion. Sean was right there, leaning against the kitchen counter looking sulky.

'You can't be serious about just letting this go, Annabel!' Leo was saying. 'You just heard him admit that he lied to you about being sick this morning, which is bad enough . . . but then to have the brass neck to go out and meet up with Zack the second school's out . . . He's lucky it was me who spotted him and not Mr Jamieson.'

'I get what you're saying,' Mum replied. 'But it's done now. I just don't see what else you want me to do!'

'For God's sake, Annabel! It's surely not that hard to come up with *some* kind of consequence! You can't just let him bunk off school!'

Mum looked very angry suddenly, as if Leo had hit on a raw nerve. 'Hey, don't *you* start with the criticism,' she snarled. 'I've had a bellyful of that already today!'

'What do you mean, Mum?' I asked – then quickly wished I hadn't as she turned to glare at me.

'What do you think I mean?' she snapped. 'Miranda is still furious with me about your party. She says I'm obviously failing to supervise the two of you adequately and that I need to address it pronto.'

'But that's not fair, Mum,' I protested. 'The party wasn't *your* fault.'

'Yeah,' Sean agreed. 'Don't listen to Miranda, Mum. It's none of her business anyway.'

'Oh, I don't know about that, Sean,' Leo put in brusquely. 'If news of your party gets out it will be very much her business that will suffer, I should think.'

'I'm dealing with this, thank you, Leo!' Mum jumped in sharply. 'There's no need for you to interfere.'

'Oh yeah?' Leo sounded annoyed. 'Well, maybe you should make up your mind, Annabel! Because one minute you're encouraging me to be a father figure to the kids and the next you want me to butt out completely. You can't have it both ways. It's confusing for me and it's confusing for them!'

There was a bit of an awkward silence while they glared at each other. Then Mum swore under her breath and stormed out of the kitchen.

It was what happened next that really scared us.

Leo stormed out of the kitchen after her, but instead of following her upstairs, he slammed out through the front door without even saying goodbye.

That night I found it hard to get to sleep, and even when I did, I ended up waking up in the middle of the night in a panic. I lay awake again after that, trying not to think about Leo and Mum. I was really worried. It's like Granny says – Mum's pretty rubbish when it comes to lasting relationships. And if she didn't do something to fix this, I was terrified that Leo would leave us for good.

Leo wasn't there when we got up the next morning, which I guess shouldn't have been surprising, though I have to admit I'd been really hoping he'd come back at some point during the night. Mum hardly even looked at us while we ate breakfast, and for the most part she seemed lost in a world of her own. I knew she was feeling down, and probably upset about Leo, and usually if she feels that way she'll talk to Miranda about it when she gets to work. But thanks to us, she couldn't even do that at the moment.

'You know, I'm really sorry about the party, Mum,' I said earnestly, feeling guilty for letting my desire to impress Rafferty override everything and everyone else.

But Mum still didn't speak and I had a horrible feeling that she wasn't even listening as she carried on sipping her coffee in silence.

Chapter Twenty-Four

It turned out to be another miserable day at school.

First I had to lie to Leo in front of our whole registration class, when he asked me why my brother was absent yet again. (Sean was taking another sick day without even telling Mum and he was planning to spend it at Blossom House.)

Priti was still ignoring me, and Lily was wandering around flanked by Clara and Hanna like they were her bodyguards. My first lesson of the day was maths (my least favourite subject) and straight away the taunts started:

'Hey, Sasha! Your mum must be pretty hot if she's going out with Mr Anderson!'

'Her mum *is* pretty hot! I've seen her!'

'So how did they meet, Sasha? Did they see each other across the room at parents' night and have that whole *lurve* at first sight thing?'

As most of the class started laughing I stood up to escape the room – just as Miss Benkowski walked in. My legs felt wobbly and my head was spinning and it wasn't a lie when I told our teacher I felt sick.

As I took some deep breaths and tried to calm myself in the girls' toilets, I vaguely wondered if this was how it felt to be bullied. Right from when I was little I'd been told I should always report bullying, but I wasn't sure if this counted as that. And even if it did, there was no way I was putting myself through the humiliation of reporting it to Miss Benkowski, who would almost certainly rush off and tell Leo.

'Of course it's bullying,' Zack said when I told him about it at break time. 'If people made fun of you for having a disability, you'd say it was bullying, wouldn't you?'

'But I don't *have* a disability!'

'Well, I'd say you've got a pretty major *social* disability,' Zack replied matter-of-factly. 'Until all the fuss dies down at any rate.'

I guessed he had a point. In any case, I was so grateful to him for looking out for me that I didn't even mind when he started up a conversation about stick insects.

'So where's Sean today?' Zack eventually asked me. 'Did Leo murder him yesterday or what?'

'Not exactly. What were you two doing in the pet shop anyway?'

'Buying some frozen mice. I gave one to Sean to use as bait. Didn't he tell you?'

I shook my head.

'We'd been talking about how to catch Monty and he mentioned that birdcage you found. Sounds just the thing, so I told him how he could use it as a snake trap.'

'I don't know why he didn't tell me,' I said crossly. 'I'm going to text him right now and see what he's doing . . .'

It turned out that Sean hadn't managed to get inside Blossom House today after all, because the gardener was there. Now he was back at home feeling worried because apparently Leo had already sent him two extremely stern texts as well as leaving an irate message on his voicemail.

I immediately sent Sean a jubilant text back: *Bet he comes round 2 check up on u after school* ☺ *!!!*

And OK, so maybe the smiley face was a bit tactless, but I was just so relieved that Leo still cared enough to keep hassling him.

But Leo didn't actually come round after school that day, or send my brother any further messages.

By the time Mum got home from work Sean was worried enough to confess straight away that he had played truant, saying he just couldn't face all the fuss about her and Leo. Luckily, instead of being angry, Mum just nodded and said that she wasn't feeling much like facing the world right now either. Then she said she was going upstairs to have a rest and to do some yoga before Leo got here later on tonight.

'Leo's coming here later?' Sean and I both said at once.

'Yes. He phoned me earlier. He wanted to pop in after school but I told him to come later once the two of you are in bed. This way he and I can have a proper talk without you two listening in.'

Sean and I looked at each other anxiously. We'd both known Mum long enough to realise what was likely to happen. Mum wasn't capable of just 'talking'. Not about this sort of thing. There would be a massive row, and tears. Mum would tell Leo to get lost. Leo would slam the door and go back to being just our teacher. Mum would be miserable again, Sean would miss Leo even more than Married Michael, and as for me . . .

'Sean, we have to do something,' I blurted desperately when Mum had gone upstairs. But even as I said it I knew there was nothing we could do but let the whole thing play out.

'It's up to them, not us,' Sean murmured, sounding just as upset as I was. 'But she's daft if she thinks we're not going to stay awake until he gets here, so we can listen.'

I was coming out of the bathroom after my much-later-than-usual shower, when I heard Leo's voice downstairs. Sean was already in position, seated on the top stair in his T-shirt and pyjama bottoms, listening intently.

'What's going on?' I whispered.

'Leo got here ten minutes ago and they're already having another row – a bad one.'

I sat down next to him and asked nervously, 'What about?'

'Us.'

Sure enough I could hear Mum's voice from the living room sounding angry. 'Leo, there's no way *you're* going to be making any decisions about *my* children! And if you think that us getting married automatically makes *you* head of this family, then think again!'

'Come off it, Annabel! That's not what I think and you know it!'

'Good, because frankly I think you're a bit too *young* to play the role of patriarch, don't you?'

I gasped and Sean let out a whispered, 'Ouch!'

Leo's voice sounded stony. 'You really don't get it, do you? I *know* I'm too young to be their biological father . . . well, not unless I'd had them when I was seventeen, God forbid.' He paused and his voice sounded shakier as he continued, 'But when . . . if . . . we get married I'll still be the closest thing to a dad that those two have got! So if you're saying you don't think I can make the grade as a half-decent step-dad because I'm too young, then maybe we *should* think again. Because there's *no* way I won't be wanting to take a role in their upbringing over the next few years!'

'Oh, really?' Mum sounded sarcastic.

'Yes – *really*. And don't look at me like that, Annabel, because from what I've seen, you could use the help!'

'Oh!' Mum sounded like she'd been slapped.

'Uh-oh,' Sean whispered.

Downstairs we heard a clatter and saw something small and shiny bounce out on to the wooden floor of the hall.

'There goes the engagement ring,' Sean muttered.

Two seconds later Mum came storming through the hall like a whirling dervish, heading for the stairs. And us.

Sean and I quickly scrambled to our feet, but we weren't quick enough. We just had time to flatten ourselves against the wall to let her pass.

'You two should be in bed!' Mum snapped as she rushed past us into her bedroom and slammed the door shut behind her.

Down in the hall, Leo was picking up Mum's engagement ring and placing it on the hall table. He looked dazed.

'Leo!' I called out hoarsely.

He looked up at us then, clearly trying to pull himself together enough to say something normal. 'You heard your mum. Go to bed.'

But we didn't move.

'Hey!' His voice was instantly softer as he said, 'I'll see you both at school tomorrow.' He gave my brother an extra long look as he added, 'Right, Sean?'

And I didn't miss the way Sean swallowed really hard before croaking, 'Yes, Leo.'

The teasing about Leo and Mum continued at school the next day, although in the light of what had happened the night before I felt a bit removed from it. As usual, neither Lily nor Priti joined in, but they both kept out of my way.

Sean and I had agreed not to tell anyone yet about Mum and Leo splitting up. I felt like I was walking round in a daze and I was afraid that even the smallest word of sympathy would make me burst into tears.

I met up with Sean and Zack in the library at lunchtime, where I listened while they discussed how to catch Monty. The snake trap they intended to set up sounded simple enough. All they needed was the birdcage and a dead mouse to put inside it as bait.

'I don't see how it's going to work though,' I said with a puzzled frown. 'I mean, Monty can get in *and* out again through the bars, surely?'

Zack just grinned. 'Come to Blossom House with us after school today and I'll show you. We can swing by your place first to pick up the mouse, right Sean?'

Sean shook his head. 'No point. Gardener's there again. I checked.' He saw the look I was giving him and added, 'It's in the freezer – in the ice-lolly box.'

'Oh my God, you are totally gross!' I exclaimed, but he just laughed.

'Let's go back to mine after school,' Zack suggested quickly. 'You can come too if you want, Sasha. You can meet Percy and Tallulah.'

'Thanks, but no thanks,' I said quickly. I looked at Sean. '*Someone's* got to go home and check on Mum.'

Sean looked at me warily. 'You don't think . . . ?'

'She said she was going to call in sick today,' I reminded him. 'So who knows?'

I think the really nervous feeling started to come over me as I approached our house and saw that all the front curtains, upstairs and downstairs, were drawn. Just seeing that gave me butterflies inside my tummy.

'Mum!' I called out after I'd unlocked the door and stepped into the hall. 'MUM!' I yelled again at the top of my voice. But there was still no reply.

I went upstairs and pushed open her bedroom door. The room was dark but I could see the mound under the covers.

'Mum?' I called out softly.

When she didn't reply I moved closer to the bed and pulled the cover off her head. 'Mum – are you OK?'

This time I got a grunt in response.

The closed curtains and Mum being in bed during the day reminded me of the time just after Mum found out the truth about Michael. It had gone on for weeks, with

Mum taking to her bed as soon as she got in from work or sometimes being unable to face getting out of bed at all and staying there all day.

It also reminded me of another time – a time when I was much younger, when Mum's bedroom had seemed like a very scary place, filled with crying that never stopped. The room had been off limits to us then and only Granny ever went inside.

Suddenly all I wanted was to contact the one person who had made Sean and me feel safe back then. And I left Mum and rushed downstairs to the hall, where I pressed Granny's number on the speed dial before I could change my mind.

Chapter Twenty-Five

As we sat eating dinner at the kitchen table the following evening, Sean was grinning and I knew exactly what he was thinking. Granny never changes. There was something quite comforting about the way she still fussed over Sean and me like we were little kids. But though I still liked the feeling it gave me to be babied a bit by her (not that I'd admit that to *anyone*, not even Lily) it was quite a long time ago that I stopped thinking of her as totally strong and infallible. I suppose it's just that, as I've got older, I've realised that Granny isn't always right about things, even if she does state all her opinions as if they're rock-solid facts.

Still, I was really grateful to her for calming me down last night, for speaking with Mum on the phone to assess the situation and for catching the first train she could, to arrive here by lunchtime today. Mum had taken another day off work but now that Granny was here she was up and dressed and at least going through the motions of sitting down at the table with us to eat a meal.

I had survived Mum's meltdown over my emergency phone call to summon Granny, but only just. I knew Mum was still angry with me and I had a feeling I was going to be in the doghouse for quite a while. But I certainly didn't regret what I'd done.

'You have to eat, Annabel,' Granny told her as Mum kept forking her food around her plate, making no eye contact with anyone.

'Actually I'm not hungry,' Mum said, standing up abruptly and leaving the table.

After I'd finished my own meal I left Granny and Sean to eat dessert and went upstairs, where I knocked on Mum's door and tentatively pushed it open.

I found her sitting on her bed staring at the photograph Lily had found in Blossom House. I guessed she must have forgotten to take it in to work.

'Mum, I didn't mean to upset you by asking Granny to come,' I blurted.

'So why did you?' she snapped, turning her face sharply to confront me. 'You knew how much she'd gloat when she found out the engagement was off.'

'I don't think she's gloating. I think she's just worried about you,' I mumbled. 'So am I, and yesterday . . . yesterday I phoned her because I was scared.'

'Scared?' She sounded surprised.

'Yes. I was scared it was going to be like the last time . . .'

'Last time? What on earth are you talking about, Sasha?'

'Well . . . it's just that when you split up with Michael you were depressed for a really long time . . . and it was scary because you didn't seem like you any more . . .' I took a deep breath. 'And after Daddy died it was even worse than that . . . and if Granny hadn't moved in . . .' I trailed off, my memories of that time so hazy that I wanted to leave them in that haze. I didn't want to remember how I'd felt peeping inside Mum's bedroom to check that the lifeless lump under the covers was still there. It was like having a body permanently in the house – only a body that wasn't completely dead. In fact I remember Sean creeping up to her motionless form one time and prodding her in the back to check if she was still alive – and both of us getting a terrible fright when she gasped and suddenly sat up.

Mum was staring at me now. Was it possible that she

was finally getting it? Getting how scared Sean and me had felt back then, I mean? Because I was pretty sure she hadn't been in any state to even notice it at the time. 'Oh, Sasha . . .' she murmured.

I found myself going to give her a hug. I'd never blamed her for collapsing. I knew how much she'd loved our dad. It was just quite hard sometimes that she couldn't seem to see that we'd actually lost *her* back then as well – and for such a long time.

The two of us stayed together like that for a little while, just holding each other, not speaking.

'I'm sorry I scared you,' she murmured into my hair. 'And that I wasn't always there for you.'

'It's OK, Mum.'

'No, it isn't.' Mum's eyes were watery as she pulled back from me and looked at me sombrely. 'But this isn't like those other times . . . I promise.'

I nodded. 'I see that now.' Because if it *was* I knew we wouldn't even be having this conversation.

'It can't have been easy for you at school this week,' Mum murmured thoughtfully as we continued to sit there on her bed.

I nodded again. 'The whole school's talking about you and Leo. They don't even know yet that you've split up.'

Mum frowned. 'Leo said it was Lily who told every-one. But it really doesn't sound like her to give away something you told her in confidence. Have you actually *spoken* to her about it?'

'No way am I speaking to her ever again, Mum! I don't even *care* why she did it – I'll *never* forgive her!' My voice cracked and I started to cry.

'Oh dear.' Mum looked a bit fazed. I guess it's quite rare for me to cry in front of her. Usually when I feel upset I figure she's got enough on her plate without me adding to it. After a few moments of awkwardly stroking my hair, she asked, 'Well what about Priti? Isn't she supporting you?'

'Priti's fallen out with me too. She's angry because I told Lily about Leo and I didn't tell her. She's spending all her time with Jillian now.'

'Well, that won't last,' Mum said briskly. 'Jillian's a nice girl but we all know she isn't best friend material, bless her.' She looked thoughtful. 'Perhaps you should approach Priti with some sort of peace offering, Sasha. I remember once I upset Miranda so badly I thought she'd never get over it. In the end I sent her a box of her favour-ite chocolates, a huge bunch of her favourite flowers and I wrote her an extremely grovelling little note as well.'

I sniffed. 'Did it work?'

'Oh yes. Mind you, her favourite chocolates were these luxury Belgium pralines that she always got from Harrods. Cost me a fortune!'

I smiled. Actually Mum had given me an idea. 'Can I go round to Priti's house tonight? I know it's a bit late but I've done all my homework for tomorrow . . .'

Mum was already nodding. 'There's a box of chocolates in the cupboard if that helps.'

'Thanks, Mum, but I've got something else in mind.'

'OK, but before you go I want to show you something.' She went to pick up a photograph album that had been lying closed on the floor by her bed. It was her own album – one with snaps from her childhood. She opened it at the first page. 'This is my parents on their wedding day.'

I took it from her, smiling as I saw Granny as an attractive young woman wearing a long, white, lacy wedding dress, standing beside my grandpa.

'Look,' Mum said, placing the engagement photo from Blossom House on the page beside it. And I had to agree that my grandfather bore a striking resemblance to the young man in the photo, though it must have been taken about ten years later.

'Have you shown Granny yet?' I asked.

'Not yet.'

'You should, Mum. It's weird. It's like there's a link between Blossom House and Granny that she hasn't told us about.'

'I'll show her tomorrow. Now go. You'd better not leave it too late if you want to see Priti.'

The look on Priti's face when I turned up at her house that evening wasn't especially welcoming, but that changed when I handed her the parcel I'd made up for her.

'Here, this is for you! To prove that you're very important to me – even if I haven't been making you feel that way recently,' I said in a rush.

Priti gasped in surprise when she discovered the red dress inside. 'You really want me to have this?'

'Yes,' I said, hearing my voice tremble a little as I added, 'I just want us to be friends again. I've really missed you. I've been such an idiot, Priti.'

In response Priti gave me a hug and told me that she had missed me too.

'Thanks,' I said, 'but you know I'll understand if you don't want to hang round with me at school until all the gossip dies down.'

'Don't worry about that, Sasha. Of course I'll hang out with you.' And she immediately started gushing about how Leo was the best teacher she'd ever had. 'I just can't believe he might actually *be* there at your house when I come round to yours. I'll get to *see* him outside of school and *chat* to him about books and . . . and . . .'

'Discuss poetry with him across the dinner table?' I suggested with a grin.

And as she gave a delighted giggle I really wished I didn't have to tell her the bad news.

Chapter Twenty-Six

The next day at school Priti stayed by my side, even though it meant getting picked on along with me. I didn't so much as look at Leo during registration and I tried to completely avoid him for the rest of the day. To be honest, the teasing about Leo and Mum had started to subside. And Priti kept her promise not to breathe a word to anyone about Mum and Leo's falling-out.

'You must be feeling upset that they've split up,' she said sympathetically as the two of us stood together in the playground.

'It's stupid really,' I said. 'I mean, I probably should've seen it coming. None of Mum's relationships ever last . . . But somehow with Leo it seemed different . . . and I was starting to hope . . .'

'Listen, we have to think positively,' Priti said. 'OK, so

they've had this terrible row! But if they still love each other then maybe they'll sort it out.'

I sniffed. 'Oh, I don't think that's likely to happen.'

'Why not?'

'Because Mum never sorts things out. When her relationships end, they just . . . well . . . *end.*'

'You shouldn't be so pessimistic, Sasha. Maybe this time will be different. My mum and dad have a big row about once a month. They shout and then they don't speak for a bit, and then Dad buys her flowers and Mum cooks him a special dinner, and then it's all OK again. Leo and your mum might still get back together . . . and even if they don't . . . well . . . maybe that's a sign that it wasn't the right thing for any of you.'

'You know, you're beginning to sound just like Lily,' I interrupted her with a weak laugh. I got a horrible twisty feeling in my stomach even saying Lily's name. We still hadn't spoken. This was the longest we'd not talked to each other since we were about five.

'What's wrong?' Priti asked me.

'Nothing,' I said quickly, knowing I couldn't tell her that I was missing Lily – not unless I wanted to upset her when she'd only just become my friend again.

*

236

When I got home after school I was surprised to find Mum sitting cross-legged on the living room floor, staring at photographs.

'What's wrong, Mum?' I asked, because I instantly knew that something was. For one thing, she was never usually home this early. 'Did you show that photo we found to Granny?'

Mum looked up at me and that's when I saw she had been crying. 'Oh yes. I showed her this morning. She said she didn't think the man in it looked all that much like my father.' She scowled and I knew there was more to come. 'So I took it into work today and gave it to Miranda. It turned out she actually had a photograph album she was keeping for the owner – one that got left behind in the house. She had it in the office so she got it out and showed it to me. There were more photos like that one in there, so there's no doubt it was a picture of the couple who lived in Blossom House. But then at the back of the album I spotted this . . .' She picked up another photograph that had been lying beside her on the floor. 'Miranda let me bring this one home to show Granny . . .'

She handed it over and I saw what had to be another picture of the young man from the engagement photo.

237

Only this time he was dressed as a magician in a red waistcoat and purple cape, and he was holding a top hat with a rabbit inside. It was obviously a publicity shot of some kind.

'So this has to be the old lady's husband a few years later,' I said.

'The thing is,' Mum continued. 'This one is *definitely* a photograph of my father. I know because I've actually got a copy!'

I stared at her, totally confused. 'Huh?'

'See for yourself!' Mum pointed behind me to where her own photograph album – the one she had shown me the evening before – lay open on the coffee table.

I went over to look and straight away I saw the identical photograph staring up at me.

'But I don't understand,' I mumbled. 'What does this mean?'

'It means,' Mum said tensely, 'that my father and the man who lived at Blossom House must have been the same person. My father was basically leading a double life – when he wasn't at home with us, he was living at Blossom House with his wife and son.'

'But that's impossible!' I protested. 'Granny was his wife!'

'Apparently not legally,' Mum said. 'This afternoon she told me the truth at last. She said that when she married him she had no idea, but he already had a wife and child. God knows how, but somehow he must have managed to set up a fake wedding.'

'But isn't that –' I broke off, not entirely sure *what* it was, apart from clearly being very wrong.

'It's a criminal offence called bigamy, Sasha. Granny only found out when he died, and she decided not to tell anyone – not even me. Since I was away travelling at the time it was easy enough for her to cover it up.' Mum's eyes were filling with tears now. 'At the time she told me she'd scattered Dad's ashes in the park. Turns out they buried him in a graveyard just down the road from here. Apparently she nearly had a fit when she realised your dad and I were looking at houses in this neighbourhood when I was expecting you and Sean.'

'But this is . . .' I broke off. I didn't know what to say. 'No wonder Granny freaked out when she saw the pictures of Blossom House,' I murmured.

Mum nodded. 'Granny told me this afternoon that she actually went there on the day of my father's funeral. Only a handful of people were at the funeral – both wives, which must have been very strange! The first wife

239

already knew about my mother and me. Granny says she was a tiny, pixie-like little thing, extremely eccentric . . . and she was wearing that dress you had on the other day because it was a favourite of my father's apparently. After the ceremony Granny was invited back to the house with the lawyer to discuss the will. The other wife spoke to my mother quite kindly. Her son was there too and they asked after me and even invited us to stay in touch if we wanted. Granny declined of course.'

My head was spinning with all this unexpected and unbelievable information. 'So the old lady's son . . . the owner of Blossom House . . . Miranda's friend . . . he's your *brother*?'

'My half-brother . . . yes.'

'Wow . . . So does he know about you? That you work for Miranda, I mean?'

'I don't know. Miranda's going to talk to him and find out a bit more for me.'

'Mum, where's Granny now?' I asked, suddenly realising that she hadn't appeared the whole time we'd been talking.

'Oh, well, Miranda gave me the afternoon off so that I could speak to her before you two got home. I must say I managed to stay quite calm until she told me my dad was buried in a graveyard just down the road from here. Then I told her she'd had no right to lie to me for all these years. She tried to say she was protecting me. I said she had just been protecting herself as usual and that in any case she'd been blind not to see at the time what was going on with my father!' Mum sniffed. 'I said a lot of other things . . . things I've bottled up for years. Anyway, then she packed her things and left. Again.'

'Oh, Mum . . .' I didn't know what to say. 'Poor Granny. How must she have felt discovering that her husband had lied to her all those years?'

'Well, she's had plenty of time to get used to it, keeping it secret from *me*! And to think she was so mean to me about Michael!'

I didn't say anything, but Granny hadn't been mean to Mum about Michael – she'd been there for us like she always was when Mum fell apart. But Mum was in such a bad mood with Granny that I knew it wouldn't help to defend her.

'Anyway,' she continued, 'Miranda's going to tell Greg. That's his – my half-brother's – name. I wonder how he'll react to the news.'

'I can't believe this, Mum,' I said. 'The owner of Blossom House is actually our uncle! How weird is that?'

I frowned as I thought about everything she had told me. 'And the weirdest part is *us* ending up living just one street away. I mean, you didn't even *know* this area when you moved here with our dad, did you?'

Mum shook her head. 'Granny and I lived on the other side of town. I'll tell you something though, Sasha. When your dad and I started looking around here for a house to buy, your granny did her best to put us off. And the bossier she was about it, the more I felt like doing the exact opposite! I'll tell you something else as well. I vaguely remember, when I was very young, my dad taking me to see some friends of his – a lady and an older boy who lived in a very big house. I even have some fuzzy memories of a garden with a lot of blossom. I think maybe my dad used to take me to Blossom House sometimes when I was very small.'

My mouth had fallen open at this revelation. 'Does Granny know?'

She shook her head. 'And I don't intend to tell her. She's already furious enough with my father as it is! Promise me you'll keep quiet about that, Sasha.'

'Don't worry, Mum,' I said. 'I won't breathe a word to anyone.'

Not even Lily, I thought. Then I remembered. Of course I wouldn't be telling Lily.

Suddenly Mum's phone rang.

'That's Leo,' Mum said, looking at it without answering the call. 'I was so upset when I found out about my father this afternoon that I phoned him in a bit of a panic and left him a message asking him to call me back.'

'Then talk to him, Mum.'

'I don't think I need to any more. I feel a bit better now I've talked to you.'

'Mum!' I reached out and grabbed the phone from her hand and before she could stop me I was speaking into it. 'Hi, Leo. Mum's right here. She's had a really big shock today and she needs to speak to you. I'll just hand you over.'

I gave Mum the phone and left them to talk while I went to the kitchen to make us both a cup of tea. Maybe Priti was right. Maybe they'd work it out after all.

Chapter Twenty-Seven

The following morning, which was Saturday, I got up at
six o'clock to use the bathroom and couldn't get back to
sleep again.

Everything was happening so quickly that my brain
was fizzing. The night before, Mum had told Sean all
about her dad and after discussing it for a while Sean and
I had decided to call Granny to make sure she was OK.
She insisted that she was but she'd definitely been a bit
frosty with us.

Leo had come round to see Mum just after Sean and I
had gone to bed. I could tell he was still here because
Mum's bedroom door was closed and Leo's washbag was
back on the shelf in the bathroom.

On my way back to my bedroom I peeked into my
brother's room to find him sitting on his bed, fully
dressed, tying up the laces on his trainers. 'Sean, where

are you going?' I asked in surprise, because he was never usually up this early.

'Blossom House.' My brother and Zack had already gone round there after school the day before, to set up their snake trap for Monty.

'I'm coming with you,' I said. 'Just give me a minute to get dressed.'

'Well, get a move on. I don't want Mum and Leo waking up.'

'You saw he stayed the night then,' I whispered. 'Do you think this means they're back together?'

'Who knows?' Sean did his best to sound casual but I could tell that he was every bit as hopeful as I was.

'You know, I really don't get the point of that cage,' I said as we closed the front door carefully behind us and set off along our road. It was pretty chilly and I quickly did up my jacket. The only other person we could see on our street was the milkman.

'How do you mean?' Sean asked.

'Well, OK, so Monty will slide in through the bars to get to the mouse . . . I get that bit . . . but then he'll just slither right out again, won't he?'

'Will he?' Sean gave me a quizzical look.

Then it dawned on me. With the mouse inside him

Monty would be too fat to squeeze out through the bars again.

'Of course!' I exclaimed. 'That's wicked!'

'In more ways than one,' Sean agreed with a grin.

'So does Zack think he's still in the house somewhere even though we haven't seen him for all this time?' I asked. I had to admit I'd been starting to think he must have escaped outside by now.

'Zack thinks he might have been sleeping under the floorboards somewhere. He says it'll be cold for him without any heating, especially at night, and that snakes tend to be less active when they're cold.'

'Well, last night was a bit colder than it's been since we got back from Greece,' I pointed out. 'We actually had the heating on, remember?'

'Yeah, well that's the thing. So did Monty!'

'*What?*'

'It was Zack's idea. He said if we made that room really warm then Monty might go back there. And that he might smell his dinner and realise he was hungry and . . . hey presto!'

'HEY!' Suddenly we heard a voice behind us and we looked back to see a bare-footed Leo standing on the pavement in front of our house, wearing a T-shirt and a pair of jeans. He'd clearly just got out of bed. I felt a gush of warmth at seeing him.

Sean and I gave him a quick wave, then looked at each other. I could tell we were both thinking the same thing. Sean glanced down to check what I had on my feet.

'Cool,' he said when he saw I was wearing my trainers instead of my flip-flops. 'Come on.'

And without looking back we broke into a run.

Five minutes later we were letting ourselves in through the back door of Blossom House. It felt different, knowing that our grandfather had lived here. As if maybe we had a right to be there.

'It's not very warm in here,' I said.

'It *will* be in the bedroom. The whole point is to entice Monty back in there, so we turned *that* radiator on full blast and switched off all the rest.'

I followed him upstairs and held my breath as we entered the front bedroom – which *was* lovely and warm compared with the rest of the house.

'Oh!' Sean exclaimed excitedly, as he stopped dead right in front of me.

'Oh, wow!' I gasped. There was Monty – his head and the top part of his body (complete with mouse-sized lump) – trapped inside the cage, while the rest stuck out through the bars.

'Monty, Monty, Monty!' Sean rushed over to kneel on the floor beside the snake, fumbling to unhook the cage door.

I watched my brother carefully move the cage round to allow Monty's upper body, complete with mouse-sized lump, to slip out through the wider opening of the door.

'Is he all right?' I asked anxiously. 'He's not hurt, is he?'

'Not that I can see,' Sean replied as he gently stroked the snake's coppery brown back. 'Monty, where have you *been*? Have you any idea how worried we've been about you?'

Just then we heard a car door slam and I went over to the window to look out. 'It's them,' I told my brother.

We had expected this of course – just not quite so soon.

'Now we're for it, I suppose,' Sean murmured. 'Still ...' He gave me a grin as he added, 'Mission accomplished, eh?'

And it seemed like nothing could spoil his good mood as he draped Monty carefully round his neck.

*

Leo arrived upstairs first. He took one look at Sean with Monty round his shoulders and let out a terrified, 'OH MY GOD!'

'It's OK, Leo. We're looking after him for Zack,' I explained quickly. 'Don't worry – he's not poisonous.'

'And you know that *how?*' Leo rasped.

'Because he's a python,' Sean answered – a bit too smugly in my opinion. 'Don't worry, Leo. Ball pythons have very friendly personalities – especially when they've just eaten.' And then he started jabbering on about how Indiana Jones was scared of snakes too, and that it was nothing to be ashamed of.

'Stop showing off and put that thing away, Sean!' Leo barked as we heard Mum coming up the stairs.

Mum let out a piercing scream the instant she spotted Monty and even Leo had a hard job trying to get her to calm down.

'I'll just fetch his box from the shed, shall I?' I said, trying not to grin as I darted out on to the landing. 'Don't worry, Mum . . . Sean will explain everything!'

I took as much time as I dared fetching Monty's box and by the time I got back upstairs again, Sean had just finished explaining to Mum and Leo how Monty had come to be there, how he'd escaped and how we had just managed to recapture him.

'For God's sake, Sean! What were you *thinking*?' Mum burst out, just as I came into the room and placed the container down on the floor.

Sean didn't reply as he knelt down carefully and concentrated on making Monty comfortable again inside his temporary home.

'Why didn't you raise the alarm as soon as he escaped?' Leo demanded. 'We could have called in the RSPCA!'

Sean looked self-conscious. 'It wasn't that simple.'

'I suppose what complicated it was your concern about what would happen to *you* if anyone found out!' Mum said sarcastically.

Sean's cheeks were reddening. So were mine. After all, Mum was right. We *had* been too concerned with protecting our own skins to think about what was in Monty's best interests. He'd had to survive without food, water or heating for all this time, whereas if we'd confessed at once and let Mum call in an expert, he might have been recaptured immediately. Then again, Zack *was* a snake expert. Not that Mum was likely to find that reassuring.

Mum spoke again, sounding very angry – and not just out of concern for Monty's wellbeing. 'Didn't you *realise* the risk you were taking agreeing to hide that snake here, Sean? You could have ruined Miranda's business! At the very least you could have lost me my job! I mean, just *how* long did you think you could keep sneaking in and out of here without being spotted?'

'We were very careful, Mum,' I reassured her rapidly before Sean had a chance to answer. Because, frankly, I wouldn't put it past him to blurt out that we'd been sneaking in and out of Blossom House for two years now with no problem at all.

Mum left the room abruptly after that, saying she was going downstairs to turn off the heating. She also told us she was going to read the gas meter and that the heating bill for last night was coming straight out of Sean's allowance (when he actually had one again).

Leo immediately started ringing up animal rescue centres, leaving messages on answer machines. Then he phoned a reptile sanctuary that was about an hour's drive away from where we live. Finally someone answered and we listened as Leo explained the situation.

'So you'll take him? That's fantastic!' Leo sounded hugely relieved as they discussed the details.

As Leo ended the call, he saw the look on my brother's face and said, 'Sean, that snake will have a very good home at this reptile place. You should be pleased about it, not sulking.'

'I'm *not* sulking. I just wanted to keep him a bit longer, that's all! I mean we only just got him back! And he's not really even my snake, he's Zack's.'

'Well, if you behave yourself I might take you to visit him.'

'Seriously?' Sean sounded disbelieving.

'Yes, seriously. So long as I don't have to touch any snakes, I think I'll cope. Now . . . I'm just going to phone Zack's parents.'

'Wait! Leo, you can't do that! They don't even *know* about Monty,' Sean protested.

'Even more reason why I should tell them,' Leo replied crisply. 'They clearly need to have a talk with Zack about the correct procedure for rehoming a python.'

'But, Leo, they're really strict! They're going to *kill* him!' As Leo raised an eyebrow, he added, 'OK, so maybe not *kill* him exactly but . . . well . . .'

'Ground him?' Leo suggested. 'Cos I believe that's the next thing your mum has in mind for you two.'

'You mean it's what *you* have in mind,' Sean grumbled.

'Actually, Sean,' Mum said coolly as she came back into the room, 'sometimes all it takes is another person to put a good idea in your head and you wonder why *you* never thought of it in the first place!'

Sean was still a bit sulky with Leo as we walked home. (Mum had stayed behind to wait for Zack and his dad, who were going to take Monty to the reptile centre.)

'I still think you could have let us keep Monty for a few more days so we could try to find him a home nearby,' he said.

'Oh yes? And exactly *where* did you want to keep him, Sean?' Leo replied impatiently. 'Because there's no way *I'm* living in the same house as a python, even if it is called Monty.'

It took a moment or two for what he'd said to sink in.

'So are you and Mum officially back together then?' Sean asked, trying his best to sound casual. 'I mean, *properly* back together – as in being an actual couple again back together?'

I could feel my own heart beating faster as we waited for Leo to reply.

'Your mother and I spent a lot of time talking last night,' he told us. 'And yes . . . we agreed that we really do want to be together and to make things work for all of us.'

Sean's immediate ear-to-ear grin was actually quite sweet. Not that I'd dare tell him that.

He quickly got a grip on his enthusiasm and grunted in a laid-back voice, 'Well, maybe you shouldn't get married *too* quickly. You could always just live together . . . loads of people do . . . and there'd be less pressure. For one thing, we wouldn't actually *be* your step-kids, so you wouldn't need to feel so responsible for us. Not that *Sasha* would be any bother of course, but as for me, I guess it's true that I *can* act a lot like a five-year-old at times –'

'Listen, Sean,' Leo interrupted him quickly. 'I said a lot of angry stuff after I caught you at that party. Maybe I wouldn't have freaked out quite so much if I hadn't arrived to find you trapped inside that airtight box . . .' He paused. 'Or if I hadn't started thinking about how the story was going to be round the school in no time and how I was going to have to give a report to Mr Jamieson, who was bound to ask me what I was doing there. Anyway, I guess I just got a bit worked up about the whole thing.'

I think Sean was probably just as surprised as I was by what Leo was telling us. Yes, I knew Leo had been totally stressed out by having to rescue Sean from that box. But it hadn't entered my head that we'd also put him in an awkward position at work and with his boss.

'Sorry, Leo,' I said with a frown, adding in a rush, 'We're really glad you and Mum are back together. Aren't we, Sean?'

'Yeah – it's a first all right,' Sean readily agreed.

'A first?' Leo looked puzzled.

I was puzzled too, until I realised what my brother meant. Basically, this getting-back-together thing had never happened to Mum before, at least not with anyone she'd broken up with since our dad died.

No wonder my brother was starting to grin. So was I.

'I should never have asked you guys to hide Monty at Blossom House,' Zack said when we saw him later that day. He and his dad had stopped at ours on their way home to let us know how they'd got on at the reptile sanctuary.

As the adults talked in the kitchen, Zack showed Sean and me some pictures he'd taken on his phone.

'He is *such* a beautiful snake,' Sean murmured as he flicked through all the photos of Monty. 'Even Sasha thinks so, don't you, Sasha?'

'His *skin* is beautiful,' I quickly agreed.

Zack looked pleased. 'A lot of people don't appreciate how beautiful snakes are, Sasha. I've got this great book about pythons at home. I bought it to try and convince

Mum that they make good pets, but you can borrow it if you like!' He gave me a very warm smile.

It was then that I remembered what Lily had said before about Zack, and for the first time I started to feel uneasy. I mean, what if Lily had got it right after all? What if Zack *did* fancy me?

I told myself quickly that it couldn't be true! But what if it was? And what if anyone at school found out?

What if Raffy found out?

I started to panic. I couldn't help it.

'Sasha, you should come round to mine and meet Percy,' Zack was saying enthusiastically. 'He's got especially strong markings for a corn snake. And he's *super* friendly.'

'Hey, Sasha, you'll be the first girl Zack's ever taken home to meet the reptiles,' Sean teased, giving me an evil smirk. 'You know ... *Meet the Parents* ... *Meet the Reptiles* ... Get it?'

That's when I started to panic even more. I wanted to be friends with Zack, but that was all. And I certainly didn't want my brother stirring things up.

I took a deep breath and heard myself say, 'Actually, Zack, I keep thinking how Monty's skin would make a really lovely handbag. Or maybe even a nice pair of shoes.'

Poor Zack looked like he'd been shot.

'She's only joking, Zack,' Sean said at once.

Seeing Zack's face, it was all I could do not to blurt out that of course I was joking, and to remind everyone that I'd refused to speak to Granny for a whole month after she'd confessed to still owning a genuine mink coat. But somehow I managed to hold it together and walk away with a totally straight face.

After all, I couldn't back down now, could I? Not if I wanted my Cruella de Vil impersonation to have the desired effect.

Chapter Twenty-Eight

For the next two weeks Sean and I were both grounded, Lily and I kept ignoring each other at school, Leo and Mum were a hundred per cent back together, but Mum and Granny still weren't speaking. I could see how happy Mum was to be back with Leo, but it made me really sad to think of Granny on her own. Sean and I both phoned her again to make sure she was OK, and she said she was. We told her all about Monty, about our friends, and I even told her about how embarrassing school had been since everyone found out about Mum and Leo. But it took us ages to persuade Mum to phone her.

Eventually, however, Mum disappeared upstairs and made the call.

'How did it go?' I asked as she came back down.

'Not too badly considering,' Mum replied. 'Though I think it's going to take us a while to get back to normal.'

'Did you tell her the wedding's back on?' Leo asked.

Mum nodded.

'So what did she say?'

'She said, "Well, dear, I suppose one good thing about him being so young is that at least he isn't already married to someone else!"'

As I winced, Sean pointed out with a little smirk, 'As far as we know.'

'I think that's the closest you'll ever get to Granny saying sorry,' I said.

It was then that I noticed Mum's new engagement ring. (The day after her row with Leo she'd tossed the first one in the bin and by the time she'd thought better of it, the refuse collection had already been.)

'Wow!' I exclaimed. 'That's gorgeous, Mum!' She held her hand out so I could look more closely. It looked a lot more expensive than the one Leo had bought her in Greece. In fact it was even bigger than the one my dad had given her, which she kept in a box in her drawer and said that I could have when I was older.

Mum smiled. 'Leo gave it to me last night. It was a complete surprise!'

'So much for treasuring the original one forever no matter *how* cheap it was!' Sean teased.

'Sean, stop being such a smart alec,' Leo told him gruffly.

I kept gazing at the new ring, letting its significance properly sink in. 'So you two really *are* going to get married,' I murmured.

And though I hadn't meant it as a question, Leo answered me anyway. 'As far as anyone can be sure of anything,' he said levelly, 'then yes, Sasha ... we really are.'

I don't know why, but that made me feel happy and sad at the same time. I was truly happy for Mum, and for Leo as well, and for all of us. But deep down inside, a bit of me still wanted to believe that my dad was the love of Mum's life, and that nothing would ever change that. Of course it was possible that he still was ... Or if Leo was, then maybe that was OK too. Perhaps our dad would have wanted Mum to find true love and happiness again with somebody else.

In any case, I was certain of one thing. Our dad would be pleased to see Sean getting the father figure he needed at long last. And I'm pretty sure he'd be ecstatic to know I was going to be stuck with some dad-style overprotection just as I entered my teens.

*

That afternoon Leo took Sean and Zack to visit Monty at the reptile centre. Mum had gone out shopping, which meant that I was alone in the house. Just as I was thinking of calling Priti to see if she wanted to come over, our doorbell rang.

I was really surprised when I looked through the spyhole and saw Ellie standing there.

'Hi, Sasha, is it OK if I come in and talk to you for a minute?' she asked in a nervous rush as I opened up.

'Sure.' I found myself feeling equally anxious as I let her inside.

'Listen, I think there's something you should know,' she blurted as soon as the front door was closed. 'It *wasn't* Lily who told everyone about your mum and Mr Anderson. It was Rafferty!'

I don't know what I'd expected her to say, but it certainly wasn't that.

I frowned. 'No way!'

'Yes, Sasha! He overheard Lily talking about it to their mum. He told one of his mates and that's how it ended up being spread round the school. Lily was going to tell you in PE that day, but you didn't give her a chance. After that she got really stubborn and said that if you thought *that* little of her, then maybe the two of you shouldn't be friends.'

'But –' I broke off abruptly, feeling a little bit sick.

'You should go and talk to her, Sasha,' Ellie said. 'You guys have been friends for ages, right?'

'Yes, but . . . but . . . I haven't spoken to her for three weeks. I guess she probably doesn't *want* to be my friend any more after –'

'She *does* want to be your friend,' Ellie reassured me, adding swiftly, 'Well she *thinks* she doesn't, but she's kidding herself because she's been really moody ever since you two fell out. Listen . . . I'm on my way round to her place just now. Why don't you come with me?'

I frowned. 'I don't know, Ellie . . . I mean, what would I say?'

'Just tell her the truth . . . that you're sorry you didn't believe her and that you know now that it was Rafferty who told everyone. Come on, Sasha . . . I know she's sorry too. Just come with me and talk to her.' As I kept hesitating, she added, 'You know, I had to leave *my* best friend behind when we moved here. You're lucky you've still got Lily.'

I looked at Ellie as she worriedly chewed on her thumbnail while she waited for me to decide what to do. It was sweet of her to want Lily and me to make up, I thought. After all, she could have used our falling-out to her advantage and tried to turn Lily into *her* new best friend.

I took a deep breath. 'OK then,' I said.

And I picked up my keys and my jacket before I could change my mind.

Chapter Twenty-Nine

I stood away from Ellie, to one side of the front door, as Lily opened it and greeted Ellie enthusiastically.

'Hi there! I was just going to phone you to see where you were –' Lily broke off as she spotted me standing there nervously.

'Sasha wants to talk to you, Lily,' Ellie put in quickly. 'I'll go and wait for you in the garden.'

Lily stared at me after Ellie had disappeared into the house. For one awful moment I thought she was going to keep me standing on the doorstep. But then she stepped back to let me through. 'I was just getting a drink,' she mumbled. 'Do you want one?'

I nodded. 'Water, please,' I said hoarsely. My throat and mouth were bone dry.

As Lily led me into the kitchen, I said, 'I'm sorry I thought it was you who told everyone about Mum and Leo.'

'You know it was Raffy?'

'Ellie just told me.'

She handed me a glass of water and said awkwardly, 'I kept checking my phone all the time thinking you would text me or something.'

'I'm sorry. Mum took our phones away after the party. We only just got them back.'

'Oh . . . that sucks.'

'Yeah.'

Through the kitchen window I could see Ellie basking on the grass in the spring sunshine.

I took a deep breath. 'Lily . . . listen . . . I'm *really* sorry I blew up at you before when you tried to tell me about Raffy.'

'Yeah, well, it wasn't very nice,' she agreed. 'It wasn't so much *what* you said, it was *how* you said it. You said it like you hated me!'

'Oh, Lily . . . I'm so sorry . . . but you know I don't hate you, right?'

'I guess you wouldn't be here if you did.'

'Well, no . . .' I paused, wondering what else I could say. 'I don't know how I could ever have thought it was you who . . .' I trailed off, not wanting to repeat myself.

'Well, you weren't exactly thinking straight at the

time,' Lily replied, 'what with everything that was going on, I mean.'

'I guess . . . but I still shouldn't have taken it out on you.'

She nodded as if that was also true.

I briefly wondered if she was going to apologise for anything herself – for inadvertently letting Raffy overhear my secret in the first place, for instance. It seemed not. Still . . . Lily was Lily and you couldn't have everything.

'Sasha, I've really missed you!' she suddenly burst out, throwing her arms round me in a big hug. 'I don't want us to fall out ever again! No matter what happens, let's definitely stay B.F.F.L.s, OK?'

'Definitely,' I agreed, hugging her back. Because even I know that B.F.F.L. means Best Friends for Life.

'Hey!' She suddenly pulled back from me. 'Are you actually wearing a *bra*?'

Before I could reply, Rafferty sauntered into the kitchen heading for the fridge. 'Is *who* wearing a bra?' he demanded.

And this time when I went bright red, it definitely wasn't because I fancied him.

*

'Sasha, just for the record, *I* think it's really cool that Mr Anderson is dating your mum,' Ellie said, as Lily and I joined her in the garden.

'That's what I keep telling her!' Lily said enthusiastically. 'I mean, he's only *the* cutest teacher in the whole school!'

'I know. And have you noticed how he always has such fresh breath when he leans over you to check your work?'

I made a mental note to tell Leo that one since I knew he'd be pleased. He always says there's nothing worse than a teacher with halitosis.

I listened as Lily described her grand plan to put a positive spin on the whole Mum and Leo fiasco at school. 'Trust me, Sasha, if handled correctly, this situation has the potential to rocket you to the very top of Helensfield High's social hierarchy! And believe me, we are talking the dizzy heights here!' She frowned as she saw the looks on my face and Ellie's. 'What's so funny?'

'*You!* Honestly, Lily, you are such a T.D.Q.!' I said.

She looked perplexed. 'T.D.Q.?'

Ellie gave me a grin to show she was with me on this. 'Total Drama Queen!' we burst out together.

'Hey, I am *not* a drama queen!' Lily protested, but she started to grin too. 'Well . . . maybe just a bit.'

Later that afternoon I was in the kitchen trying to rub an ice-lolly stain off the front of my T-shirt when Rafferty suddenly walked in and stood in front of me awkwardly. I couldn't help noticing how muscly his arms were but I felt a lot more detached about that fact than I usually did when the two of us were in such close proximity.

Before I could muster up my best glare and tell him to get lost, he began nervously, 'Hey, Sasha ...' He was chewing his bottom lip, something he used to do a lot when he was younger, and his hair was sticking up on top so he didn't look as cool as he usually did. 'Listen, Sasha ...' he began again. 'I'm really sorry ...'

I just about fell over on the spot! Raffy was *apologising* to me? I mean, was I hallucinating this or what?

'I know I shouldn't have told Jake about your mum and Mr Anderson,' he continued rapidly. 'I didn't know he was going to tell everyone, but still ... it was dumb.'

'Yeah, it *was* dumb,' I agreed coolly.

He sighed. 'Look, if it makes you feel any better, Mum and Dad nearly killed me when they found out. I was grounded and had to give up my phone for two weeks.'

'Yes – though I don't think that was enough of a punishment for him really,' Lily chipped in as she came in from outside.

'Hey!' Raffy protested, dodging out of her way as she picked up a hefty wooden spoon and threatened to give him a hearty whack on the bum.

'Actually, Sasha, *you* should be the one getting to do this!' Lily teased.

'Get lost, Lily,' Raffy growled. He was clearly embarrassed, judging by how he was blushing.

Weirdly enough it was right then that the funny little knot I'd had inside me ever since Ellie had told me what he'd done seemed to vanish as quickly as it had come. And, much to my frustration, there was something about seeing Raffy just a little bit vulnerable that made me like him all over again.

What was wrong with me?

Of course I knew what Mum would say if I told her, but frankly I didn't always find her whole 'hormones' explanation for everything all that comforting. Because if *this* was what hormones did to you when you were just coming up to thirteen, I doubted I was going to make it to adulthood without going completely bonkers!

Chapter Thirty

The next day Mum went round to Miranda's house (Miranda no longer blamed her for the party, thank goodness) and while she was there, Miranda introduced her to her half-brother on Skype for the first time.

'What's he like, Mum?' Sean and I asked in unison the second she got back.

'Well, actually he reminds me quite a lot of my father,' Mum said. 'He told me he remembers me coming to Blossom House a few times when I was three or four, though they didn't tell him who I was. His mother knew all along about my mother and me and told him later when he was a teenager. It sounds like his parents had rather an unusual relationship to say the least! Anyway, he says he wanted to get in touch with me years ago, but his mother always insisted he respect *my* mother's wish for no further contact. He definitely wants to meet up now though. He's coming over from Canada in a month's time. You won't believe this, but *he's* a magician too.'

'No way!' Sean blurted. 'Maybe he'll be able to teach *me*!' He grinned as he added, 'Hey, you probably don't need to bother with maths and English and all that conventional stuff if you want to be a magician, right, Leo?'

Leo just rolled his eyes and didn't reply.

'Greg's only a magician in his spare time, Sean,' Mum said. 'He's also got a degree in architecture and now he owns his own building firm.'

'So does he have a family?' Leo asked.

'He's just got divorced. No children. What's interesting is that he's asked Miranda to take Blossom House completely off the market. Apparently he's thinking of leaving Canada and moving back here and, if he does, he'll probably want to live in Blossom House while he renovates it himself. Miranda thinks he's also very keen to get to know us.'

'Hey, you should totally invite him to the wedding, Mum . . . seeing as how he's your brother,' Sean suggested.

'Half-brother,' Mum reminded him sharply. 'And of course I'm not inviting him. Think how Granny would feel.'

'Are you sure Granny's definitely going to *come* to the wedding?' I asked her with a frown.

'Oh, I'm fairly certain she won't miss it.'

'Hey, Mum, why don't *we* offer to buy Blossom House from your half-brother after he's done it all up?' Sean suddenly said. 'We could sell this house, and Leo could sell his flat, and we could all move into Blossom House together.'

Sean's tone was light, as if he wasn't all that serious, but just the same I found myself holding in my breath. If Blossom House really did become ours it would be . . . well . . . it would be the happiest ending in the whole history of happy endings as far as I was concerned!

I looked hopefully at Mum and Leo . . .

'I doubt selling both our places would raise enough to buy Blossom House, Sean,' Leo said.

'In any case, Granny would never forgive us,' Mum added dismissively. 'And not only that – do you honestly think *I'd* ever want to live there now?'

I had to admit that I hadn't considered how Mum might feel about the house now that its connection to her family had been revealed. I must have let out a louder sigh of disappointment than I'd intended, because suddenly they were all looking at me.

'I'm sure we could find ourselves a *smaller* lovely old Victorian house with high ceilings and wooden floors and a nice big garden if we set our minds to it,' Leo said. 'Isn't that right, Annabel?'

Mum nodded. 'Absolutely. You know how much I love old houses. But I want us to move somewhere where we don't have any sort of personal history – somewhere that will give us a fresh start as a family. You do understand that, don't you, Sasha?'

I nodded. Of course I understood. It didn't mean I wouldn't miss Blossom House though.

'Hey, Sasha, you never know, maybe our uncle will want to live there himself after he's done the place up,' Sean said. 'We'd be able to go there whenever we liked then!'

'That *would* be cool,' I agreed with a smile.

'Please don't get your hopes up on that front, you two,' Leo warned us. 'It's an enormous house for just one person. I'd be very surprised if your uncle intends to move back in there permanently.'

I lifted up my chin and said stubbornly, 'Stranger things have happened.'

Leo laughed. 'Oh, in *this* family, Sasha, I don't doubt that they have.'

I briefly wondered if I ought to be offended, but when I looked at the happy smiles on Mum's face and on my brother's, I decided to let it go. After all, what did it matter if Leo thought our family was strange? He was still choosing to become one of us, wasn't he? And in *my* book that was what mattered most.

REAL WORLD. REAL GIRLS. REAL EMOTION.

THE HONEYMOON SISTERS
Gwyneth Rees

Poppy's family has always included at least one
little foster brother or sister. But when her mum
announces they'll be getting a new foster child,
she isn't expecting it to be Sadie. Sadie is hard
as nails, cold as ice, tougher than a tiger –
and she's the new girl in Poppy's class at school.
They'd never be seen together in public. Now
they're sharing a bathroom. How can Mum fall
for Sadie's sweet-as-honey act, when Poppy
knows all too well what she's really like?

Coming soon!

GWYNETH'S TOP FIVE FAVOURITE FICTIONAL HOUSES

1

MISSELTHWAITE MANOR in *The Secret Garden* by Frances Hodgson Burnett

It's not just the garden that is full of secrets.

2

MANDERLEY in *Rebecca* by Daphne du Maurier

Another house of secrets, this time with a wonderfully scary housekeeper thrown in. (This one's meant to be for adults, but I read it when I was a teenager and loved it!).

3

THE GINGERBREAD HOUSE in *Hansel and Gretel* by Hans Christian Andersen

Yum yum!

4

LITTLE HOUSE ON THE PRAIRIE by Laura Ingalls Wilder

I loved the TV programme as a kid and now I'm loving reading the books with my daughter.

5

THORNTON HALL in *The Making of May* by Gwyneth Rees

I know it's cheating to include one of my own stories. But getting to create my own house full of mysteries was brilliant fun.

GWYNETH'S TOP FIVE PLACES TO HAVE A PARTY

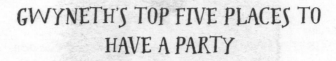

1. **In a walled garden** – preferably not a secret one or there wouldn't be many guests!

2. **In a palace** – that's the princess in me talking!

3. **On a rooftop terrace in Venice** – I have done this one for real and it was fab!

4. **On a beach** – a gorgeous, warm, tropical one preferably.

5. **In a chocolate shop** – yes, they honestly do have parties in chocolate shops!

ALL ABOUT GWYNETH!

If you'd like to find out more about Gwyneth Rees,
check out her author page on
Facebook.com/GwynethReesAuthor
or email her on **gwyneth.rees@bloomsbury.com**.

Please make sure you that you have permission from a parent or guardian.